FURY

F-BOMB: CURVY VIGILANTES, BOOK ONE

MARY E THOMPSON

BluEyed
Press

Fury

F-BOMB: Curvy Vigilantes, book one

Ebook ISBN: 978-1-953879-26-4

Print ISBN: 978-1-953879-27-1

Audiobook ISBN: 978-1-953879-28-8

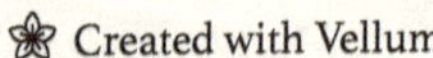 Created with Vellum

To every woman who has ever doubted her own strength... you can do anything and you are powerful beyond your imagination. Never give up.

1

Stacey Allen was not at a funeral so she could avoid her husband.

She nudged her sunglasses up her nose and ground her teeth together. Her focus never strayed from the wooden box as it disappeared around the edge of the dirt. Not many people remained. It wasn't often that people stayed to see a casket lowered into the ground. Even less common when the woman inside the casket was a ghost for the last five months.

Stacey wasn't there because they were friends. She was there out of obligation. Holly was a client of Stacey's. They talked every day for a month, then weekly for another three months. Stacey recommended Holly go back to her life. She thought the woman was healthy. She thought she was safe.

Stacey was dead wrong. And now Holly was dead.

Stacey blamed herself for Holly's death. She wasn't the one who dragged Holly from her car and stabbed her, but Stacey was the one who told Holly she would be okay.

"We're heading out," Captain Patrick said quietly.

Stacey nodded. "Thank you. I won't be long."

Captain Patrick nodded and offered her a sympathetic smile. Stacey's boss and friend, Frannie, hugged Stacey, then looped her arm through the captain's. They walked together, past the rows of stones on the hill.

Stacey tried to hold back her tears, but she was losing the battle. She was angry. Not just at herself for thinking Holly would be safe when she left the shelter and tried to live her life again, and not just at Holly's husband who was the one and only suspect as far as Stacey was concerned, even though he hadn't been charged. No, Stacey was mad at her own husband.

Wray Allen. The man Stacey fell in love with a lifetime ago. The man she planned to spend her life with. He was a good man, at least, she thought he was. But for the last six months, Stacey couldn't see that version of her husband. The only one she saw was the one who gambled away almost everything they had and nearly bankrupted them. The man who put his problems, his addiction, above the safety of his wife and sons.

One woman was dead because of the sins of her husband. Stacey told her patients they deserved better, but she never took the advice herself. She'd spent years counseling abuse victims that it wasn't their fault and that they didn't need the men who hurt them the way the men convinced them they did. Stacey empowered women to stand on their own and make a new life for themselves.

Instead of listening to her own words, Stacey was letting her past dictate her present. Her parents' divorce ruined her childhood. She hated them for not trying to save their marriage. Stacey wouldn't do the same thing to her sons. She needed to try. But trying wasn't getting them anywhere. Something had to change, and she knew what it was.

Stacey had been sitting on the sidelines of her own life,

afraid to make the leap and tell her husband it was over. Maybe it was time.

"We should get home," a man's voice said from not far away.

Stacey looked up, and her stomach turned. She'd never known hate so strong as she felt in that moment. It tore her heart out and flipped her insides and made her want to do something she knew she couldn't do. It made her want revenge.

Oscar Hyatt stared at Stacey, a triumphant look of pleasure curling his lips up. His arm was draped over the shoulders of his daughter, Vera, as Vera stared at the hole in the ground where her mother's body would stay.

Stacey wanted to rip Vera from her father's arms. She was a teenager, barely old enough to know her own mind, and she was under the care of a monster. A man who not only abused Holly, but who Stacey was completely convinced also killed her.

Except he had an alibi and was not a suspect.

"I just want to stay a little longer," Vera said. She sniffed and wiped her nose on the back of her hand. "I can't believe she's gone."

Stacey knew Vera. They'd spoken regularly when Vera lived in Shelter from the Storm with her mother. Stacey counseled both of them to help them through the situation they were in. Vera hadn't been a victim of her father's, but she knew what he did to her mother. But Oscar doted on Vera. Manipulated her to love him.

Vera leaned against her father's side, and Oscar hugged her tighter, his hand rubbing her shoulder for comfort. The entire time, he smirked at Stacey. He knew exactly who she was, and she knew he was guilty, but they both knew there was nothing Stacey could do about it.

"Vera," Stacey said softly, ignoring the cancer around the girl.

"Stacey!" Vera rushed over to her, throwing her arms around Stacey's neck and burrowing in. She sobbed against Stacey's shoulder. "Why did this happen?"

Stacey glared at Oscar. "I wish I could tell you that, honey. Your mom was a beautiful person, inside and out, and some ugly, evil person stole her from all of us."

Oscar flinched ever so slightly when Stacey called him ugly and evil. He quickly schooled his expression and sneered. It wasn't a confession, but it was enough for Stacey to know for sure he was guilty. Too bad she couldn't go to the cops with a guilty look.

"I don't know what I'm going to do without her."

"I know, sweetheart. Where are you staying?"

"With my dad. He didn't do this, Stacey. It wasn't him. And he would never hurt me."

Stacey brushed Vera's blonde hair back from her face and smiled at the trustworthy child. Vera was fourteen. Barely old enough to know her own mind, let alone understand how disgusting some of the world was. Holly was a miracle-worker to have kept her daughter so hidden from the horrors of their home, not to mention the rest of the evils of the world. Especially when that evil lived under the same roof.

"You know you can always come see me. And you can always call me. I'm always going to be here for you."

Vera nodded. "I know. Thanks, Stacey."

"Vera, we need to go," Oscar demanded.

Vera looked over at him and saw the scowl on his face. She ducked her head, then said a quick goodbye to Stacey before rushing back to her father's side.

Oscar smirked at Stacey, then guided Vera to the waiting car.

Stacey stared after them, watching the way he touched his daughter. He wasn't inappropriate, which both relieved and bothered Stacey. If he grabbed Vera's arm or did anything that made it look like he hurt the girl, Stacey would have the power to remove Vera from his care. But Oscar did nothing.

Stacey waited until they got in the car and drove away. She turned back to the grave and stared at the simple box that held Holly. Stacey closed her eyes and promised Holly that she would find proof that Oscar killed her and get Vera away from him.

She just hoped she could keep the promise.

WRAY ALLEN TACKLED his older son, Joey, and tickled him until he squealed. Evan, his baby, jumped on Wray and dug his chubby fingers into Wray's side, laughing the whole time like he was the one being tickled.

Wray pretended Evan's uncoordinated fingers were the funniest things in the world and laughed loudly. Joey jumped in and joined his little brother, both of them jabbing their fingers into the soft tissue on Wray's neck and sides. It wouldn't be long before those little fingers would hurt more than tickle, but Wray wasn't going to think about that. He was going to enjoy the time he had with his sons and hope he could fix things with his wife so he didn't miss out on more than he already had.

A car door slammed outside, and both boys jumped up.

"Mommy's home!" Joey shouted as he ran for the door.

"Wait," Wray commanded his six-year-old in the dad

voice he didn't break out often. Joey had started opening the door when he felt like it and answering the door without a parent. It didn't matter how many times they told him to wait, he never did. It was bad enough that Wray installed a video doorbell so they would always know if Joey left the house.

Joey stopped and gave Wray an annoyed look that nearly made him laugh. He held it together and cocked an eyebrow at his oldest.

"You know you're not supposed to open the door without a parent."

"But it's Mommy. She's a parent."

Wray tried to figure out how to talk around that logic and was grateful when Stacey let herself into the house before he had to come up with something.

Evan threw himself at Stacey, wrapping his arms around her legs so she couldn't get inside far enough to close the door. "Hi, Evs. Did you have fun with Daddy?"

"We tickled," Evan said in his three-year-old blabber. He'd grown a lot in the last six months. He was still a baby, but going from two to three and starting preschool were big changes. So big that Wray dreaded how much more he'd miss. His guess was, the way his wife avoided his gaze, his time on the couch was coming to an end.

Wray fell in love with Stacey the night they met. He was playing cards at a game a friend organized in college. Stacey walked in and he felt an odd buzz of energy, like a piece of his he hadn't known was missing was finally back. Her pull was magnetic, and Wray couldn't have resisted it if he tried. But he didn't want to. He wanted to know her, and as the night wore on and she indulged his claim that she was his good luck charm, Wray knew he'd never be able to walk away from her.

After the game, Wray talked her into breakfast at a local diner, paid for with his winnings, then convinced her to let him take her to dinner that night. From then on, they were together.

In the decade since, Wray had learned everything about his wife. Normally it was a blessing to know someone so well, but when the words she held back were bad, it was a curse. A curse to know his time at home was short-lived.

"Did you guys eat a snack?" Stacey asked the boys when she finally got Evan off her leg and closed the door.

"Yep. Daddy made us cheese and crackers," Joey said.

"Okay, good. Give me a few minutes to change and then we can talk about dinner," Stacey said. She made a move toward the stairs. Her black dress, black boots, and black purse would have looked a little dramatic at the party they were going to, but the mention of dinner told Wray she forgot.

"Emily will be here at five. Do you want to wait to figure out dinner until she gets here?" Wray asked. It was a gentle reminder they wouldn't be home to eat. A way for him to tell her they had plans without making her feel bad for forgetting. At least, he hoped.

Stacey hung her head. Her shoulders slumped. She looked like she might collapse right there on the stairs. "Taylor's party. I forgot."

Wray didn't reply. There was nothing he could say that would not piss her off, so staying silent felt like the right move.

"Let me change into something less formal. Yeah, we'll talk to Emily about dinner."

Wray nodded even though Stacey wasn't looking at him. Evan made a move to follow Stacey up the stairs, but Wray scooped him up and rolled him up onto his shoulders, tickling his exposed belly and making Evan squeal with laughter.

Stacey trudged up the stairs without looking back.

Wray set Evan on the floor and smiled at the wide grin on his son's face. Both boys were blissfully unaware of the tension between Stacey and Wray. One of the good things about them being so young when their parents' marriage was faltering. Wray hated it, but he was the one to blame. If it hadn't been for him getting sucked into an illegal gambling ring and nearly losing everything, he wouldn't be sleeping on the couch.

While Stacey was changing, Wray and the boys cleaned up the living room. Joey insisted on helping pull out the takeout menus to show Emily when she arrived. He told Wray Emily really liked pizza and made sure that menu was on the top.

Wray smiled to himself. His son had his first crush on his babysitter. Stacey would think it was adorable.

The doorbell rang before Stacey came downstairs. Wray let Emily in and thanked her for coming. Emily lived a few houses down from them and was a regular babysitter for the boys. She was fun and kind, but also responsible and considerate. She was always their first choice for babysitters.

Stacey hurried downstairs while Wray was talking to Emily. Stacey's eyes were red and puffy. She was still avoiding Wray's gaze. Tension coiled tighter and tighter inside him. He was running out of time.

Wray hurried upstairs and changed, then said goodbye to the boys and Emily and followed Stacey outside to his truck.

Their drive to Taylor's was quiet. Wray tried to think of what to say to her, but nothing ever felt right.

They turned onto Taylor's street, and Stacey finally said, "We need to talk."

"Now? When we're about to pull into the driveway?"

She looked through the windshield like she hadn't realized where they were and shook her head. "No. Not now. Soon."

"Okay," Wray said. His time in front of the firing squad would be here soon. Dammit.

STACEY WAS happy to be home. Not that she didn't love Taylor, but Taylor was convinced she could save Stacey and Wray's marriage. Stacey appreciated her friend's positivity, but Stacey wasn't so sure. The biggest sticking point for her was her sons, which was why she wanted to talk to Wray about making a change to their situation. She didn't know what, but him sleeping on the couch wasn't working. They didn't talk. They didn't touch. They didn't do anything. They were strangers under the same roof, pretending to be married and in love for the rest of the world.

Stacey knew living a lie was not the way to go through life.

She was so sure after Holly's funeral that ending things was the only option left, but every time she saw her husband, the idea wasn't so solid. She couldn't imagine her life without him, even if a life with him wasn't much of a life.

Wray parked the truck in the driveway and got out without a word. He hadn't tried talking to her lately. At first, he apologized at least once a day, but it had been months since he said he was sorry and weeks since he initiated a conversation about anything.

Wray unlocked the front door and stepped back to let

Stacey go through first. Even if he wasn't speaking to her, he was still the man she loved. That man was buried deep inside, but little things like that gave Stacey a glimmer of hope that if she could get past the hurt, maybe they could find their way back to each other.

Stacey unzipped her boots and set them on the rack, then hung her purse on the hook by the door. The house was quiet, telling her the boys were asleep. The TV flickered in the living room where Emily usually settled after the boys fell asleep.

Stacey walked into the living room and stopped. Instead of stretched out on the couch like normal, Emily was curled up in the lounge chair, her neck at an awkward angle. She didn't look comfortable at all.

"Why is she in the chair?" Wray asked.

Stacey shook her head and walked over to Emily. She was close to Vera's age, but the differences between the two girls' situations were shocking. Stacey wished Vera could have the stable life Emily had.

Stacey put her hand on Emily's shoulder and gently shook her, calling her name. "Emily. We're home. Wake up."

Emily stretched and blinked her eyes open. "Hey." She rolled her neck and winced, rubbing the kink.

"Why aren't you on the couch? That would have been more comfortable."

Emily shrugged. "Joey wouldn't let me sit there."

"What? Why not?"

Emily nibbled her lip. Her gaze flickered between Stacey and Wray, then settled on her hands. "He said it was his daddy's bed, and I wasn't allowed to sleep there or sit there."

"He... What?" Stacey gasped. She thought they were hiding Wray sleeping on the couch from the boys. She thought they had no idea.

"Why don't I walk you home?" Wray suggested to the silent room. It was their normal. Stacey checked on the boys and Wray walked Emily home and paid her. But nothing felt normal with that bombshell.

"Um, yeah. Thanks," Emily said. She uncurled herself from the chair and gave Stacey a red-cheeked smile, then ducked her head and grabbed her shoes.

"I'll be back in a minute," Wray said, although Stacey thought it was more for Emily's benefit than hers.

"Okay."

The door closed behind them, and Stacey sank to the chair. Joey knew. And if Joey knew, then fixing things before the kids found out anything wasn't an option. He already knew.

After a minute, Stacey forced herself to get up. She didn't want to be sitting there when Wray got home. She wanted to be upstairs, in her room, hidden from her husband.

She checked in on the boys and kissed both their cheeks. She hurried to her room and changed into pajamas. She flushed the toilet just as the camera at the front door alerted her to Wray's return. Stacey rushed to bed and jumped under the covers, turning away from the door and pretending to be asleep.

Wray came in a few minutes later. He called her name quietly, but she didn't move. He sighed heavily, then opened and closed a drawer before closing himself in the bathroom. Stacey didn't move until after he was out of the bathroom and his soft footsteps padded down the stairs.

She'd decide what to do tomorrow.

2

―――――

STACEY WOKE UP THE NEXT MORNING WITH NO MORE ANSWERS than she had the night before. Shielding her kids from what was going on between her and Wray was always her top priority, but if they knew, was she really doing the best thing for them?

She asked herself the same question as she made her way downstairs. The living room looked the same as it always did. No sign of Wray having slept on the couch. The house was quiet, the boys still sleeping, which left Stacey wondering where Wray was.

His sneakers were gone, but his truck was still parked in the driveway. She walked through the downstairs, finding a full pot of coffee and no other sign Wray had been up.

The thump of feet hitting the floor above her head sent Stacey into mommy mode. She listened for the footsteps to lead to the bathroom, then the toilet flushed and the footsteps moved toward the stairs. A minute later, Joey shuffled into the kitchen.

"Good morning," Stacey said. She hugged him as he sat at the table.

"Morning."

"Are you hungry?"

He shrugged. He wasn't a morning person and usually took a little while to wake up enough to eat or talk.

"Want to watch TV for a few minutes?"

"Is Daddy gone?"

"I think he went out for a run. I'm sure he'll be back soon."

"But you don't know?"

"His truck is here. Daddy runs a lot."

Joey grumbled something and padded back to the living room.

Stacey leaned against the table and tried to make sense of what was happening with her family. She stayed with Wray to keep her family together, but the tension between them was still hurting everyone.

Evan was up not long after Joey and joined his brother in front of the TV. Stacey fixed herself a cup of coffee and sat down just as Wray came in the front door, dripping with sweat.

"Morning, everyone," Wray said, smiling at the boys and avoiding Stacey's gaze.

"Hi, Daddy!" the boys said immediately. They jumped up but stopped when they got a few feet away from him. "Ew. You're stinky."

Wray lifted his arms above his head and stomped toward them. "I'm going to make you stinky."

"Ew! No! Gross!" Evan screamed. He ran back to the couch and hid under a throw pillow.

Joey laughed and backed up, keeping his distance, too.

Wray stopped before he stepped onto the carpet. "I'm going to run up and shower. Then how about we go play outside, boys? Let Mommy have some time to herself this morning."

"Yeah!" they shouted.

"All right. I'll be back soon. Think about what you want to do. Braden might come over, too."

The boys cheered. Wray took the steps two at a time. A minute later, the shower turned on.

"Do you boys want breakfast before you go outside?" Stacey asked them.

"Pancakes!" Joey shouted.

"Yeah, pancakes," Evan agreed.

Stacey sighed. Guess she was making pancakes. And had time to herself to figure out what she wanted to do about her marriage.

WRAY STARED at the back of the house and wondered what Stacey was doing inside. He wanted to talk to her, but he knew she wasn't open to talking. Not after what Emily told them the night before.

Wray failed all of them. He wanted to fix it, but no matter what he tried, he kept making things worse.

"You all right?" Braden asked.

Wray shrugged and pulled his attention from the house to the backyard. The boys were chasing each other, screaming and laughing. Braden was standing next to Wray and watching with him.

"I've been better."

"What's going on?"

"Just waiting for my wife to tell me she's done trying."

"You think she's going to?"

Wray didn't want to say the words out loud. He didn't

want to believe it could be true, but it was hard to imagine any alternative. It was even harder to admit it.

"I don't know. Maybe just being paranoid."

"Yeah, probably. She seemed fine when I got here."

Wray nodded, but he knew that was only because Stacey didn't like airing their dirty laundry. She believed family stuff should stay in the family. Her parents' divorce became a spectacle for the entire town when she was a kid, and she always said no one else needed to know that much about what goes on inside a family.

Joey ran over and plowed straight into Braden, looking up at him with a smile. "Are you going to play?"

Braden snarled back and started chasing him around like a wild animal out for a hunt.

Joey and Evan screamed and ran from Braden. Evan ran for Wray and hid behind his legs when Braden turned his way. "Help, Daddy."

"Daddy? There's no Daddy here," Wray said, turning to attack his youngest.

Evan squealed and took off. Wray chased him, the four of them laughing and running around the yard.

After that game, they climbed in and out of the play-house, then the boys drew pictures on the patio with chalk. The afternoon went quickly, and before he knew it, Stacey was calling the four of them in for dinner.

"Are you staying, Braden? We have plenty," she asked with a welcoming smile.

"Yeah, that would be great. Thanks, Stace."

She nodded and pressed her lips into a smile that never met her eyes. Wray watched her, seeing the tension in her shoulders and the strain on her face. She didn't meet his gaze.

Wray helped the boys get plates of food and carried

them to the table. Braden went after them. Wray turned to get his own plate and found Stacey smiling at something Braden said. Wray walked over and picked up the last plate, taking his place in their short line behind Stacey.

She looked up at him like she didn't expect to see him there. She pulled her gaze away, then set her plate back down and mumbled something about forgetting to do something and left the kitchen.

Braden looked at Wray, but all he could do was shrug. Any time he was close to her, she bolted. He'd almost gotten used to it.

The five of them ate dinner with the boys carrying the bulk of the conversation. Stacey barely said a word. She stared at her plate and ate her food, then shooed them all out of the kitchen so she could clean up.

Wray hated the distance between them. With the boys occupied for a minute and Braden there to keep them distracted, Wray went back to the kitchen to offer to help clean up.

Stacey was at the sink scrubbing the pan she cooked dinner in.

"Can I do anything?" Wray asked.

She jumped, dropping the pan in the sink and splashing soapy water all over herself and the counter. She turned to glare at him and shook her head. "No. You've done enough, Wray."

"Stacey..."

"No, Wray. I am not going to talk about this now. Not when Braden is in the house and the boys are in the next room," she hissed.

Wray nodded slowly. All he wanted to do was be there for his wife. To show her he was sorry. She clearly had different plans.

STACEY GLARED at her husband's sleeping form. After the restless night of sleep she had it pissed her off to see him sleeping soundly. She wanted to kick the couch and wake him up. To dump a bucket of ice water on him. To—

"Just say it, Stace," he said, his voice thick with regret and acceptance.

She should have known he was awake. The man was a constant surprise. Like when he gambled away their entire savings account, nearly lost their house, and almost got himself killed in the process.

Not all surprises were the good kind.

"We need to talk." The words scratched out of her throat like glass shards, taking pieces of her with each word. She hated that she had to be the one to say it. That she had to be the bad guy. But he was forcing her into it.

He opened his eyes and avoided her gaze. He wasn't the man she once knew. The man she thought she knew. He'd changed. He was broken, damaged, wounded. He was not the protector she fell in love with. Her husband was gone. The man in front of her was a shell.

He sat up on the couch and faced the living room. The muscles of his back bunched and teased Stacey as she watched him. Her mouth still went dry at the sight of him, his shorts low on his hips. The smooth line of his spine was one she'd spent many nights licking. His shoulders had showcased wounds from her teeth. She loved him with every last fiber of her being, and she still wanted him, but the most important thing in the world, the thing that kept them together for almost a third of their lives, was gone.

Trust.

He stood and faced her, his bare chest capturing her

attention. The dips and peaks of his upper body tantalized her. Shadows accentuated the efforts he took with his strength. He knew it was a weakness for her. He knew she always felt like she wasn't a good fit for him. She was all plush curves to his angled lines. They didn't match, but he said they did. She believed him. And when he lifted her over his shoulder in a fireman's hold on their wedding night and carried her up and over the threshold and up the stairs to their bedroom where he spent the entire night worshipping her body, she couldn't ever argue again.

He grabbed the shirt he discarded after Stacey went upstairs the night before and pulled it over his head. He was doing it for her. Hiding the mouth-watering sight of his body so she could think straight and say what she needed to say.

Even at the end, he was watching out for her.

"I think you should move out."

He met her eyes for the first time that day. The pain and regret in his was almost enough for her to second guess her decision. She still loved him. She wanted to fix what had happened. But she had no idea how they could get back to before.

Before he betrayed her.

Before he betrayed his best friend.

Before he betrayed himself.

Finally, Wray nodded. "Okay. When do you want me gone?"

Stacey wasn't sure what to expect, but easy acceptance wasn't it. "I don't know. I didn't really have a date in mind."

"Can you give me a few weeks? I need time to find a place."

"You're going to get a new place?" she blurted.

Wray looked up at her, anger and frustration in his gaze. "I'm not sure what else I would do. I figured that's the best plan."

"Oh. Um, okay." She wasn't sure what to say. Or what she wanted. It hurt that he was willing to just accept her choice and move on. She wanted him to fight. She wanted him to push. She wanted him to want her the way she still wanted him.

But he didn't. He just accepted what she said. So, she had to do the same.

"I'll get the boys up. If you're okay with handling their morning," she said.

"Yes. And I'll get them to school today like we planned. We'll figure out how we're going to balance their schedules when I'm gone."

Stacey nodded. She stared at the couch again, wondering if she'd burn down the entire house if she set the couch on fire. All the good memories of when they bought it and christened it the first night were gone. She only saw her husband sleeping on it...because she couldn't stand to let him in their bed.

WRAY WATCHED Stacey walk away and had to fight himself to stop from begging her not to kick him out. He'd known it was coming, but he still hated it. When she found out the truth about his gambling, she was pissed. When she found out the full extent of it, how many times he'd lied and how much money he'd lost, she couldn't even look at him.

He couldn't look at himself either.

Wray hated himself for what he did to Stacey. And his

best friend, Braden. And his kids and the rest of his family and friends. Not everyone knew the full story, but the few who did thought he was the lowest scum of the earth for it.

They weren't wrong.

And that was why he couldn't beg Stacey to change her mind. He'd been sleeping on the couch for six months. Six months since she admitted she couldn't stand being in the same bedroom as him. Six months since she kicked him out of their bed. Six months since he held her.

He didn't deserve her. He should be in jail. He was lucky all he lost was her respect. He assumed she would have kicked him out immediately, but she didn't. She tried to move past what happened, but she couldn't. It was too big for her to forgive. He knew he'd lose her eventually.

"Time's up," he muttered to himself as he folded up the blanket he used. He put it on the back of the couch like Stacey liked. He put his pillow in the ottoman and fluffed up the cushions so it was less obvious he'd made them his home.

Not that he was fooling Joey.

The boys came racing down the stairs, shouting for breakfast. Wray smiled. He wouldn't have survived the last six months if it weren't for his kids. They were everything to him, after Stacey. They were quick to forgive and forget, too.

Wray helped Joey with his cereal, holding the end of the jug while his son poured the milk into the bowl. He wanted to be a big boy. Wray tried not to think about all the things he would miss. Mornings like that where they were being silly and childish and little boys.

Stacey came into the kitchen dressed for work. She wore black pants that hugged her curves and a loose, blue blouse that floated around her then settled on her breasts. Before he messed up their lives, he would have wrapped his arms around her and nibbled on her neck and told her how beautiful she was. He always loved the way she looked in blue, how it brightened her eyes. But he couldn't say things like that anymore. She was done with him.

Stacey said goodbye to the boys and left with only a nod for Wray. For a long time, he worried their sons would notice that things had changed between them. Until two nights ago, when Emily told them Joey refused to let her on the couch, Wray thought the boys were oblivious. They didn't notice much of anything if it didn't have to do with them. But Joey knew. And both boys would know everything when Wray didn't come home.

Wray finished breakfast with the boys and hustled them upstairs. He helped both boys brush their teeth and had them in the truck and buckled into car seats on time. Stacey was not a fan of lateness, and Wray had learned not to deliver the kids late to school.

Joey was the first drop off. Wray pulled up into the loop for his school, pausing to let a family walk through the line of cars. Wray stopped when it was his turn and made sure Joey was okay getting himself out of his seat.

"Bye, Daddy. Love you!" Joey called as he pushed the door open, barely letting Wray stop the car before he was racing after his friends and running into school with them.

Wray watched him until a horn behind him told him he needed to get moving. He checked his mirror and started moving.

"I lub Miss Stephie," Evan said on the way to his preschool.

"I know, bud," Wray said. "She's pretty great."

"She give me cookie."

"Oh, really?" Wray was pretty sure she wasn't supposed to give the kids food that wasn't parent approved.

"Yeah. For hers bird-day."

"It was her birthday?" Wray clarified. Stacey had an ability to make sense of everything the kids said and anticipate what they needed. Wray never figured out the baby talk or the toddler ramblings.

"That what I said."

"Oh, well, cool. Did you have a party for her at school?"

"Yep. Today. We bringed ice cream."

"We did?" Wray asked. He didn't remember Stacey mentioning ice cream, although he didn't hear much after her telling him to move out. Maybe Evan was wrong. Stacey didn't normally forget things. It was unlikely she would have forgotten this.

"Yes. Mommy says so."

"Um, okay, then. If Mommy said so, then we brought ice cream."

Wray parked and opened the back door to get Evan out of his seat. He grabbed his backpack and happily trounced across the parking lot, only held back by the hand Wray held tightly to. He signed Evan in and walked down the hallway to his classroom, saying hello to the teachers and parents he recognized.

"Good morning, Evan," Miss Stephanie said when they reached her door. "How are you today?"

"Good," he said, hugging her around the middle. "It your bird-day."

"It is my birthday. Are you excited for our party?" Miss Stephanie asked. She gave Wray a friendly smile, then focused right back on Evan.

"I am. Mommy said we bringed ice cream."

"Ooh, well, thank you. Your daddy can put it in the

freezer down in the cafeteria." She swung her eyes to his. "Do you know where that is?"

"Um, yes, but I don't have ice cream. Stacey and I must have gotten our wires crossed this morning. She didn't mention it. I'll have to bring it back." Wray felt like a crappy father, but that was a feeling he was definitely getting used to.

"You forget?" Evan said, his voice loud in the already loud hallway. "Why you forget? Mommy said!"

"I'll get it, buddy. She just forgot to tell me about it. Don't worry. I'll bring it back."

"But you forget!" Evan howled. He burst into tears and turned to Miss Stephanie. She put her hand on his back and patted it.

"It's okay, Evan. We have lots of treats for today." Miss Stephanie gave Wray a look that was part apology and part dismissal. She couldn't have been much older than twenty, and she still had him feeling like a chastised child.

"I'll go get it right now. I'll be right back. It'll be in the freezer when you have your party. I promise." Wray had his keys out and was going to walk away when he realized he hadn't said goodbye yet.

"I love you, Evan. I'm sorry I forgot. I'll fix it."

"You didn't fix it with Mommy," Evan said, pulling back from Miss Stephanie's leg long enough to shoot Wray a glare that had him rocking back and wanting to run. Guess both boys knew.

"I'll fix everything, Evan. I promise."

Evan gave him a look that said he knew Wray was full of shit and went into the classroom. Wray was left standing there with Miss Stephanie, wondering how to explain what just happened.

"Good morning, Alexis," she said to another student.

The look on her face was bright and cheery, and she slid Wray a glance that said she knew far too much.

He simply nodded and walked away. It seemed everyone knew he sucked as a father and a husband and, in general, just a man.

Maybe ice cream could fix one of those.

3

———

Stacey sat at her desk and tried to focus. Telling Wray to leave was harder than she thought it would be. She expected a fight, or a plea, or something. Instead, she got acceptance.

She was trying for the same thing. She felt like she was the only one holding on to their marriage. Maybe if she accepted it was over, she could move on and not feel so horrible about it ending.

It was hard to do, and for the first time, she understood how her clients felt. Stacey hadn't been through what they went through, but it was harder than she ever thought it would be to let go of a dream she'd had for ten years. To say goodbye to a person she thought would be in her life forever. And to admit she was no better than her parents.

She told her clients all the time that letting go was usually the hardest part of moving on with their lives. As a domestic abuse counselor, she worked with women looking to sever ties with their abuser permanently. Many were women who had gone back to an abusive husband or boyfriend more than once, but they decided they were ready to end things. Stacey was the one who helped them to do that.

She loved her job, but there were definitely things she hated about it. Seeing the same women in her office again and again reminded her that abuse was a cycle. Women didn't fall for abusive men. They fell for amazing men who were kind and caring and wonderful. Men who had excuses and explanations and accusations at the ready whenever they struck out. The ones who went back, went back because they trusted the first man, not the second. Some worked out, but most did not.

"Are you ready?" Frannie asked with a quick knock on her door. Shelter in the Storm was Frannie's brain child. She opened the doors six and a half years ago, and Stacey was grateful every day for the chance to help Frannie and the women who came for help.

Stacey nodded to Frannie. Frannie stepped back and let Raina in, then closed the door so they could have privacy for their session.

Raina was a repeat client. She was a strong, stunning woman who ended up with the wrong man. She went back to him after her first stay in the shelter because he convinced her he hadn't meant to hurt her. Her second stay in the shelter started with a fractured orbital and three broken ribs. Raina vowed never to return to him.

Stacey stood and welcomed Raina into her office. Raina was a petite, curvy woman with caramel brown hair that swayed a few inches past her shoulders. Her hazel eyes were kind and watchful, and her posture had changed in the few weeks she'd been at the shelter. She was confident and strong, and she was going to be fine on her own.

"Hi, Raina. How are you?" Stacey asked. She hugged the

other woman, a gesture that helped clients to acclimatize to positive physical contact.

Raina returned the hug warmly and held on for an extra few seconds. "I'm great. I finally feel like I can stand on my own two feet. And I have you and Francesca to thank for that."

Stacey shook her head. "You did the hard work. We just helped you to see you could."

Raina drew a breath, her chest expanding as she accepted the words into herself like Stacey taught her. Her shoulders sagged with relief, and she nodded. She was ready for her new life.

"Have you heard from Damon?" Stacey asked. Distance from the ex was always part of the plan, especially when he was a repeat offender.

Raina shook her head. She picked at her unpainted nails. "I know he's still looking for me, but he doesn't have any way of getting in touch with me."

"What is your plan going forward? How are you going to stay away from him when you're not here?"

"I'm going to live with a friend. She's been great to me through all of this. She is the only one I've been in touch with, and she knows everything. She doesn't want me alone, so she offered to let me live with her."

"That sounds like a good plan. It's always good to have people in your corner, especially people you trust and who will protect you." Stacey thought of her own life. She knew Wray would protect her if she ever needed it, but trusting was a different story. A part of her felt like a hypocrite for telling her clients all these things and not living them in her own life. But it made her see she deserved better. Her husband wasn't physically abusive, but he wasn't a great husband to her either. Not over the last six months, or before.

"Next time, see if your friend can come in here with you. I'd like to meet her and help her understand ways to help you. I also want her to know she can call me if either of you ever needs anything."

"Okay, sure. Karli probably won't mind that."

"Good. Tell me what else is going on."

Raina launched into the rest of the session, and before they knew it, their hour was up. Stacey hugged Raina again and let herself believe she would be one of the success stories.

She checked her phone for any missed calls or texts. She kept it on silent during sessions so she wasn't interrupted. When she saw a missed call and three missed texts from Wray, her traitorous heart leaped.

Stacey opened the text messages and scowled when she read them.

Wray: I didn't realize we were supposed to bring ice cream for Miss Stephanie's birthday today. Evan is upset. Going home to check the freezer. Sorry I forgot.

Stacey winced. She forgot to tell him about it.

Wray: Found an unopened Neapolitan. I'm guessing this is it. I hope so. Sorry if I took the wrong thing.

Stacey nodded to herself. He was correct. But she felt bad for making him go through an extra trip.

Wray: Ice cream has been delivered. Hopefully Evan can forgive me.

Stacey: I'm sure he will. Sorry I didn't mention it earlier. That was what I bought for today. Thanks for doing that.

Stacey stared at her phone a minute longer. Wray didn't reply to her text. It was irrational to want him to, but texting was the most communication they had lately.

A knock on her door had Stacey tucking her phone away again. Frannie stuck her head in and glanced around. "Doing okay?"

Stacey nodded. "Yeah. It was a good session."

Frannie opened the door and walked in, closing it behind her. She took the seat Raina vacated minutes earlier, settling her tall, plus-size figure into the comfortable chair. "Raina seems to be healing finally. I hate when it's that bad. I wasn't sure she was going to survive that first night."

Stacey nodded. She saw Raina the day after and she wasn't sure how the woman had survived the night. "Thankfully, she did. And she's doing well."

"Good. How are you doing?" The look in Frannie's hazel eyes was one of kindness, not judgement, but Stacey felt the judgement, anyway. She knew what Frannie was really asking about.

Stacey busied her hands by sorting through the stack of mail she'd been neglecting. Most of the time it was junk, so she never bothered to deal with it on a schedule. She couldn't remember the last time she went through it.

"I'm good," Stacey lied. In the middle of the stack was a plain white envelope. There was no return address, but the stamp said it was mailed locally.

"Are you sure?" Frannie asked, her tone telling Stacey she didn't believe her for a second.

Stacey pressed her lips into a smile and opened the envelope. She didn't get a lot of mail, and definitely didn't get many handwritten letters. She didn't recognize the handwriting. She flipped the page over and gasped.

"What? What is that?" Frannie was up out of her seat and rounding Stacey's desk before she could answer.

"It's from Holly."

"Are you sure?"

Stacey clapped a hand over her mouth and flipped back to the beginning to read Holly's words.

Dear Stacey,

I'm sorry to be dropping this on you, but you and Francesca are the only ones I know I can trust. You two and my neighbor who's sending this if something happens to me. Which means if you're reading this, I was right. And now I'm dead.

God, this is harder than I thought it would be. A part of me knew if I stayed with Oscar, he would kill me eventually, which was why I left. Living at Shelter in the Storm for so long made me stronger. It changed my life. I would have gone back to him if it weren't for you and Francesca. And God knows what would have happened to Vera.

If I'm dead, you have to prove that he did it. Not because I want him to go down for something he didn't do, but because I know he's following me. I don't know how he found us, but he did. I saw him. He disappeared when I looked, but I know it was him. And if he's following me, he's going to come after me.

Please protect my daughter. Don't let Vera stay with him. Don't let him hurt her. I know you and Francesca will help. He's an evil man. When we first met, he wasn't as bad, but he's not that man anymore. He's evil. I won't rest if he has my daughter. Please help her.

My everlasting gratitude,

Holly

Stacey reread the letter four times before she processed the words. Stacey knew Oscar was guilty, but she had no proof. If he was following Holly, that had to be worth something.

"Wow. I mean, I'm not surprised, but wow." Frannie walked to the other side of the desk and sat down. She leaned forward, her elbows on her knees.

"What can we do? Should we call Marcus?"

Frannie looked up at Stacey like she'd grown a second head. "Why?"

"Because it says right there that Oscar was following her. He killed her."

Frannie sighed and folded her hands in her lap. "Stacey, we can't do anything about that. It's not proof of anything."

"Are you saying he's going to get away with it?"

"He has an alibi. He didn't kill her."

"You know that's not true. He was involved. He had to have been. Maybe it was like Strangers on a Train or something. He and a friend killed someone for each other."

"Honey, you know we can't go around saying that."

"Why not? He killed her. It's too convenient that he was following her, then she ends up dead. He would have killed her before if she hadn't come here."

"I know. Holly was lucky she got out of there when she did. And I really thought she was going to be okay."

"She should have been. He followed her and killed her. We need to call Marcus."

Frannie sighed again. "You can call him, but he can't act on this."

"Why not?"

"They've already cleared Oscar. If they go back at him with something like this, something unsubstantiated, he can sue the police department for harassment."

"It's not harassment if he's guilty."

"It is if there's no proof. If there's no new evidence that says he could have done it. That letter isn't evidence."

Stacey wanted to scream. Or cry. Or something. He was going to get away with it. Unless they found proof. "What if we find proof?"

"Like what?"

"What if he confesses?"

"It still has to be proven. A confession is only one piece of evidence. It's a strong one, but it's still only one."

"What if we prove his alibi wasn't real?"

"That could give cause to look into him again, but there weren't any cameras in the area where Holly was killed. Her car was torched a few blocks away, and it never went through any street cameras. There's not a lot of evidence."

"I can't give up."

"I didn't say you should. I'm just not sure what you're going to find. If you find anything."

"I have to try."

"Are you sure you're doing this for the right reasons?"

"Is there a wrong reason to prove someone is guilty of murder?"

"Not if he actually is. Is everything okay with Wray? You seem more on edge than normal."

Stacey thought about lying to her boss, but Frannie knew the whole story. Captain Patrick was her husband and was involved in the case that set Wray free and exposed his secrets.

"I asked Wray to move out."

Frannie closed her eyes. "I'm sorry to hear that."

Stacey shrugged and tried to hold back her tears. "Me, too. I have been holding on for the boys, but apparently they know we're having trouble. And nothing has changed between us. I still love him, but I can't be with him if I can't trust him."

Francesca nodded. "No, you can't. And if neither of you are going to do anything to change that, it's better for both of you to end things now, so maybe you can find a new happy ending."

"I've tried to change things," Stacey argued.

"You have?"

"Sure. I'm trained. I know what to do. He just won't listen to me."

"And you know you can't be objective when you're one of the clients."

Stacey sighed and glared half-heartily at her friend.

Frannie laughed and stood. "You can get upset with me if you want, but you know I'm right. And you know Wray is a very good man. He messed up, and I'm not going to say he didn't, but he has taken whatever you've thrown at him for months. Maybe you guys should try to be less civil and get it all out."

Stacey pursed her lips and stared straight ahead while Frannie moved toward the door.

"I'm not sure having a shouting match is a good idea. Ugly things come out when people do that."

"Ugly things stay buried when people don't," Frannie countered. "I don't know the answer. I don't have the degree or the experience helping people through something like what you're going through. All I know is when Marcus makes me mad, we get it all out in the open and say the things we need to say, then we make up like bunnies and all is right with the world."

Stacey snorted. "I really don't think sex is going to fix our problems."

"Maybe, maybe not. But it's a damn good way to try." Frannie waved and let herself out of Stacey's office. "Let me know if you need any help with the Holly stuff. And be careful."

Stacey nodded at Frannie's back and debated her advice. Yelling at Wray didn't seem like the right thing to do, but if it got them past the strain and to a place of healing, maybe it was worth a shot. It was a much better idea than having sex. Not that Stacey didn't miss sex with her husband, but sex was more than just physical for her. She liked to look into his eyes and see him. Connect with him. Know he was the only man who would ever make her feel the way he did.

It all felt like a fantasy now. She'd barely been able to be in the same room with Wray for months. Being in the same room and getting naked and touching each other was beyond what she could imagine. Even if she had imagined it many, many times over the months.

God, she wanted him still, but she couldn't forgive so easily. Not when she couldn't trust him. When she couldn't trust herself with him.

She couldn't fix her marriage, but maybe she could figure out what really happened to Holly. Get justice for a woman who didn't deserve to die.

Stacey nodded and grabbed the letter from Holly and read it again. She took a picture and saved it to her phone and computer, just in case something happened to the letter.

Time to do some research.

4

———

Wray saw the text from Stacey, but he didn't answer it. Saying anything felt natural, normal, and not right anymore. He needed to figure out how he was going to move on from her and let her go like she deserved. As much as he hated the idea.

"You done?" Braden asked, drawing Wray's attention from his phone and back to the weight room.

Wray shook his head and switched places with Braden on the leg press. Workouts were a part of the job for firefighters, and even when they were off duty, they could use the gym. It came in handy on days when your wife asked you to find a new place to live.

Braden stared at Wray while he lifted. The look on his face made Wray more than a little uncomfortable. They were getting back to the easy friendship they'd had forever, but Wray knew it would never be the same. Not after Braden was dragged into Wray's mess.

Wray got in over his head with the gambling. He let it get out of hand. At first, it had been about earning a little extra money to help pay off some of their debts, but it quickly became more for him. He spiraled toward addiction and found himself unable to stop, even when he knew he was in far over his head. When the people in charge of the game offered to forgive his debts if he brought in a new player, Wray debated the choice. When they said they'd take out his debts on his family, Wray had no choice but to do as they said.

Braden didn't like being a pawn, but he understood that Wray was doing what he could to protect his family. Stacey was far less understanding. Wray didn't blame her.

"What's going on with you today?" Braden asked.

Wray looked up at his friend and realized he'd been sitting on the machine without using it for a long minute. Wray jumped up and wiped it down, ignoring the question.

"Did something happen with Stacey?" Braden pressed. He didn't meet Wray's gaze, but Wray still felt the weight of it on him.

Wray sighed. Braden was his closest friend and the only one who knew everything about what happened. Braden was like a brother to Wray, and Braden's siblings, especially his oldest sister Taylor, were like family.

"Stacey asked me to move out."

"Whoa. Seriously? When?"

"This morning. After Taylor's party Saturday night, the babysitter said Joey wouldn't let her sit on the couch because it's my bed. I think that was the last straw for Stacey."

Braden's brown brows shot up. "You didn't say anything yesterday. I thought you were keeping everything from the boys."

Wray nodded. "Apparently we weren't doing as good of a job as we thought. Even Evan said something this morning about it. That I didn't fix things with Stacey."

"Called out by a three-year-old?"

"Yeah. Talk about a great parenting moment. But he's right. I've been on the couch for months. Whenever I try to talk to Stacey, she's not interested. So, I quit trying. Months ago. Nothing is going to get better if we don't talk."

"Want me to take the boys so you can talk?"

Wray sighed. "I don't know. I don't know if she'd even talk to me."

"Well, if you want me to take them, I will. Where are you going to go?"

"I need to find a place. Never thought I'd be looking for an apartment at thirty-one. Especially alone."

"Do you really need an apartment? Why don't you stay with me?"

Wray shook his head. "She asked me to move out. She's done. Moving in with you feels like hoping she'll change her mind, and I'm kind of out of hope."

"You're completely out of hope? Because that's not the man who made Stacey fall in love with him. Who didn't give her the choice to say no. Who fell for her the night you met and decided she was yours forever."

"I'm not sure if he still exists."

"Then you better fucking find him. Because you have an amazing wife who is hurt. You hurt her. You broke her trust, and you made her doubt. You put your entire family in danger because you were selfish and stupid. You need to own up to that shit and grow a pair and get your wife back. Because I promise you, if you let her go, someone else is going to swoop in. Stacey is too good of a woman to go unnoticed and stay single."

"What the fuck are you trying to tell me?" Wray growled at his soon-to-be-former best friend.

"I'm telling you, you're an even bigger dumbass than I

already thought you were if you walk away from your wife and kids. Do you know how many men would love to have what you have? Would love to come home to someone else?"

"So what, you're going to make a move on my fucking wife when I move out?"

Braden rolled his eyes. "You're an idiot. I'd never go after Stacey. All I'm saying is if you still want to be married to her, you need to make sure she knows she's the most important person in your world and you'll do anything to keep her. If you don't want to do that, be prepared for someone else to."

Wray grumbled under his breath, but he knew Braden was right. Stacey was too perfect for other men to not notice her. Her curves and her brains and her devotion to their family were only some of the reasons Wray loved her. And instead of fixing what was wrong, he was acting like she'd wronged him by not immediately forgiving him. He was the fuck-up, and he needed to start going big or he was never going home again.

WRAY SPENT the rest of his day trying to figure out ways to apologize to Stacey and win her back. The most important thing in her life was their family. But being a good father and husband wasn't enough after the epic failure he was.

Wray picked up Evan first. He walked into the preschool and down the hallway, the noise of kids getting ready to leave echoing through the tiled space. Most of the time, Evan stayed for afternoon day care, but on days Wray was available, he always picked him up to have more time together. He hoped it was a good idea after the birthday party debacle.

"Daddy!" Evan shouted, running across the room to Wray. "You bringed the ice cream!"

Wray smiled and rubbed his son's curly blond hair. "I did. I told you I would."

"Tank you."

"You're welcome. How was the party?"

"It was great! Miss Stephie said it was her bestest bird-day party ever."

"Well, I'm sure that's because all of you are such amazing little people."

"Yep. I tink so, too."

Wray smothered his grin. "Should we get your stuff?"

"Yep," Evan said. He skipped to where his backpack hung in the hallway. He zipped it up and threw it over his shoulder, then smiled up at Wray.

"Are you ready?"

"Yep."

"Did you say goodbye and happy birthday to Miss Stephanie?"

He nodded, then walked to the door and shouted, "Bye, Miss Stephie! Happy Bird-day!"

"Thank you, Evan! See you tomorrow." She waved at Wray to acknowledge she saw him, then turned back to the remaining students.

Evan trotted down the hallway, telling Wray all about what they did at preschool that day. He was still chattering when he was buckled into the car and they were on the way to Joey's school.

Joey jumped in the car and buckled his harness. Wray checked that it looked good, then pulled into the flow of parents leaving the school.

"How was your day, Joey?"

"Good. Can I go over to Adam's house this weekend?"

"I don't know. We have to talk to Mommy."

"What if she says no?"

"Then I guess you can't go."

"Why not?" Joey whined.

"Mommy hasn't said no. Why are you getting upset about this?"

"Because I really want to go."

"Okay, and we'll talk to Mommy tonight."

"Fine. What's for dinner?"

Fucking hell, is he a teenager? Wray fought the urge to roll his eyes at his oldest. He'd gone from sweet little boy to temperamental teenager in the span of a year. Instead of a six-year-old, he was acting more than twice his age. With all the attitude that came with it.

"I don't know yet. How about we figure that out when we get home so Mommy doesn't have to worry about it?"

"I like when Mommy cooks," Joey said.

"Me, too!" Evan agreed.

"I know, but Mommy needs a break sometimes. Daddy is going to cook tonight. How about pork chops on the grill?"

"I don't like pork chops," Joey declared.

"Neither do I."

And so it continued. Everything Wray suggested was shot down by Joey, and Evan agreed with his brother. They made it home and into the house. Wray got them both to hang up their backpacks, take out lunchboxes, and start homework. With them involved, he looked through the fridge and freezer to find something he could cook for dinner. Something foolproof so he didn't mess it up and give Stacey one more thing to have to deal with.

How hard could cooking dinner be?

THE HOUSE WAS utter chaos when Stacey got home. She walked in the front door and seriously considered turning around and going right back out again.

But then Evan saw her and called out to her, and she knew she was trapped.

"Hi, honey," she said, hanging her purse on the hook and covering it with her jacket. She continued into the kitchen and hugged him, sticky fingers and all. "How was your day?"

"It was awesome! Miss Stephie had a bird-day today," Evan told her.

"I heard. It sounds like you had a great party."

"Yep."

"And you? How was your day, Joey?"

"It was fine. Can I go to Adam's this weekend? He got a new video game, and he was telling me about it. Can I go?"

"Let me talk to his mom, okay? I just want to make sure you're invited."

"Fine," he sulked.

Stacey lifted her gaze to Wray's in time to see him roll his eyes. She raised a brow at him, and he gave her a sheepish look.

"It looks like you guys already took care of dinner. What are we having?"

"Macaroni and cheese!" Evan shouted.

"Mashed potatoes," Joey said.

"And broccoli," Wray added. "And I grilled pork chops. They didn't want pork chops, but they were in the freezer and sounded good."

Stacey rolled her lips in to avoid lashing out at him. He was doing her a favor by cooking dinner, so yelling at him wouldn't help things. He didn't know she was saving the pork chops for the weekend. He also didn't know that she made a menu for dinners. Or that she had things planned out for weeks in advance.

Because he never bothered to ask. That was the way their lives worked. She took care of everything at home, and he got to be the fun parent who made macaroni and cheese and mashed potatoes.

"I guess that works," Stacey forced herself to say.

"I screwed something up, didn't I?" Wray asked.

"It's fine. I just need to rethink a few things."

"I'm sorry. I wanted to save you extra trouble. I figured you had a rough enough day today."

Stacey glanced around the house and wondered what trouble he saved her from. As far as she could tell, the kitchen was a disaster, the living room looked like a tornado hit it, and the backyard had all the outside toys strewn everywhere. She was going to need to spend an hour cleaning before she could even consider relaxing.

"It's fine."

Wray tried to hold her gaze, but Stacey looked away. She focused on the boys like she'd been doing since Wray disappeared on her. Since she thought something happened to her husband and cried her eyes out for days, only to have him show up again and for her to then find out he owed tens of thousands of dollars to some shady men because he gambled away their life savings.

Stacey sat down at the table between her boys and asked more about their days. She took a bite of mac and cheese from Evan and mashed potatoes from Joey. When Wray set a full plate in front of her, she looked up at him and thanked him.

Then immediately turned back to the boys.

Wray hung around the edges while Stacey talked to Joey and Evan and made them laugh. She ate her dinner while they ate theirs, and when they were done, she was finished, too.

"All right boys," Wray said before they'd even put their plates in the dishwasher. "Time to clean up the backyard."

They grumbled for a second, but they followed Wray outside and the three of them cleaned up the yard. She watched from the kitchen window and smiled when Wray picked both boys up and threw them over his shoulders. He ran around the yard with them and collapsed into a pile with the boys on top of him near the playhouse.

The three of them laughed and played and managed to clean the backyard eventually. By the time they came in, Stacey had cleaned the kitchen and picked up the living room. And it was time for baths and bed.

Wray herded the boys upstairs and got both of them into the tub. Stacey sat on the couch and listened to them play and talk. Tears rolled down her cheeks when the three of them laughed, Wray's deep laugh that lit up all her good parts, and the boys' smaller laughs that sounded like mini versions of their father's.

She never imagined she'd leave him. When she met Wray, she knew she'd never love another man the way she loved him. Acceptance was the hardest thing because she wanted to believe the man she fell in love with was still in there, but she couldn't find him.

The rumble of footsteps down the stairs told Stacey the boys were ready for bed. They jumped on her and hugged her, then raced back up the stairs to Wray. That had always been their routine when he was home. He wanted as much of the day-to-day as possible since, when he was working at the fire station, he was gone for at least twenty-four hours.

Stacey stayed on the couch and listened for the quiet. The soft tones of Wray's deep voice faded as he grew quieter with the story he read to them. She heard the creak of his footsteps as he carried Evan back to his own room. Then both doors closed quietly.

Stacey drew a breath and held it, waiting for Wray to come downstairs. She felt like she'd been fired from a job but had to finish the week in the office, even though she knew she wasn't allowed to stay.

Or more accurately, she was the boss, and she'd fired Wray as her husband.

His footsteps on the stairs were solid and sure. Wray stopped at the bottom of the stairs and let out a heavy sigh.

It had been a long time since she waited for Wray to come downstairs after saying good night to the boys. Usually she snuck upstairs when he read, or hid in the kitchen until he was on the couch, then hurried past him with a hasty good night and hid in her room until morning to avoid talking to him.

But her conversation with Frannie echoed through her mind. She wouldn't yell at him with the boys upstairs sleeping, but maybe she could try to talk to him. Get some of the things she wanted to say out in the open.

Stacey waited a minute for him to come around the edge of the couch and sit down, but he chose the chair on the other side of the room. Keeping his distance.

It stung like a tetanus shot. She watched him, wondering when he'd gotten older. She couldn't remember the last time she looked at him and thought of him as a stranger, but in that moment, he was.

"Are you okay?" he asked gently, as though the words wouldn't be allowed.

She supposed she deserved that since she yelled at him to stop asking her that question a month after the truth about his gambling came out. He asked her daily, sometimes multiple times a day, and she finally lost it and told him she wasn't okay, she might never be okay, and she didn't want him to ask if she was okay ever again.

Now, she sat on the couch that was his bed and stared over his shoulder at the wall.

"What's going on, Stace?" Wray asked.

"I don't know if I can forgive you," she finally admitted.

He leaned forward in the chair and clasped his hands together. He didn't respond, just hung his head.

"What you did... I hate that you put us at risk."

"I didn't know you would be until you were."

"You also lied to me. For a long time. You said you were with Braden when you weren't. Months and months of lies. Do you know how that makes me feel?"

Wray sighed and lifted his head. "No. Because you never told me."

Her gaze snapped to his. She expected cockiness or a smirk, but he just looked back at her. He was being honest, which was far more than she'd been with him.

"I hated you when I found out," she whispered. "I never thought I would hate you, but I did. It felt like you'd been cheating on me."

"I never—" The pain in his dark eyes surprised her.

"Maybe not, but I don't think that would have been worse. When you came back, I was so relieved. But when they told me what actually happened, why you were gone in the first place, I was so mad at you."

"I never cheated on you. I never even thought about it. All those times... I know I fucked up, and if I could go back, I would."

"I wish you could because then I wouldn't feel this way. When I look at you, I don't know how to feel. There's a part of me that hates you, but I also still love you. And I don't know what to do."

Wray opened his mouth but didn't say anything. He rolled his lips in and stayed silent for a long minute. "You've already decided. You asked me to move out."

She nodded slowly. He was right. Asking him to move out was a painful choice, but it was a choice. She knew she couldn't keep doing what they'd been doing. She wasn't fighting for them to stay together, but neither was he. And if neither of them wanted their relationship to work, it was better if they stopped pretending it might.

"You're right," she said softly. "You're right. I guess that's it then."

Wray nodded. "I guess so."

5

———

STACEY HAD A LIGHT DAY THE NEXT DAY, SO SHE WENT OUT FOR lunch and to drive around. She knew the police had gone over the area where Holly's body was found, and that Marcus handled the case personally, but Stacey still wanted to go there. She needed to see for herself where Holly died.

The area of the city was mostly abandoned. There were a few old warehouses there, but nothing looked open. No cars were parked on the streets or close to any of the buildings.

Stacey parked and got out, wandering across the street to where Holly's body was. The concrete sidewalk had been cleaned, but Stacey knew where she'd been thrown after she was dragged from her car. Right on the sidewalk in broad daylight. Whoever killed her knew the area was not heavily trafficked and knew they could attack her without being caught.

Stacey wiped at the tears that collected on her lashes. The last time she saw Holly, Holly was laughing and happy. She was making plans for her future. She wanted to see Vera walk down the aisle. Holly was even thinking about being open to a relationship again. One day. After Vera was grown.

Stacey had given Holly the name of a colleague to continue her therapy. Stacey only worked with women and children who lived at the shelter, but she had contacts who helped them transition to a normal life. Holly never made it to her first appointment.

A car turned down the street, coming from the opposite direction Stacey had driven. She didn't think anything of it, even though the area was deserted. As the car drew closer, the hairs on the back of Stacey's neck rose. The car crawled toward her, going far below the thirty mile per hour speed limit in the area.

Stacey turned, wondering why someone was going so slowly. She assumed they were lost. She peered through the windshield, trying to get a look at the driver, and stumbled backward.

Oscar.

He smirked at her, then gunned it, tearing down the street and making a fast right turn, disappearing around the corner.

Stacey raced to her vehicle and cranked it up. She peeled out, making a sharp U-turn and chasing after Oscar without stopping to put on her seatbelt. She grabbed the strap and tugged, locking it and having to let go. She made the same right turn as Oscar and spotted his periwinkle car up ahead. Stacey pressed the gas harder, trying to catch up to him.

When Stacey got close enough that she could follow him comfortably, she eased off the gas and stayed a few car lengths back. She was sure he knew she was following him, but she couldn't miss the chance to see where he went.

She got her seatbelt on as she merged into the city traffic near downtown. Late fall was a good time to visit Niagara

Falls, and the beautiful day brought out more than the normal number of visitors. Stacey got shuffled back, losing sight of Oscar's car in the long line on the two-lane side street.

Stacey watched at every turn to see if he went a different way, but she never spotted his light blue car. She kept following him, she hoped, into the city and closer to the Falls.

Traffic slowed as pedestrians increased. Every light required waiting for a steady stream of people to cross before anyone could go through the lights. Slowly, Stacey trusted she was edging closer to Oscar until she finally spotted his car just three ahead of hers.

The car directly ahead of Stacey turned at the next light, pausing to wait for pedestrians and blocking the lane so Stacey couldn't make it through the light. When the car turned on yellow, Stacey floored it and barely made it through the light.

Two lights later, the one car between them turned, leaving Stacey right behind Oscar. He didn't speed up or make any sudden moves. He just kept driving like he was out for a coffee run.

They got past the heaviest of the traffic and were working their way north away from the busiest part of the city. Stacey continued following Oscar as he turned down one side street after another. She wasn't entirely sure where she was, but she was getting closer to finding answers. She had him in her sights.

The road widened to two lanes in each direction, and Stacey moved over to give the impression she wasn't following Oscar. They went through one light as it turned yellow. They approached another, and the light flipped to yellow when they were too far away to make it.

Oscar sped up. Stacey panicked for a second. She couldn't lose him. She hit the gas and prayed the light stayed yellow a few more seconds. She was almost there when Oscar swerved right in front of her.

She yanked the wheel to avoid hitting his car. Her car came to a sudden stop, jolting her forward. The airbag popped out, cushioning Stacey's face as she careened toward the windshield.

She bounced back, her head hitting the seat. The car creaked and whined as it stopped against the other vehicle.

"Are you okay?" someone shouted through her window.

Stacey pushed the airbag down so she could see. Everything hurt. She reached for the door handle, fumbling when it wouldn't open before she realized the car was still in drive. She shifted to park, and the automatic locks opened so she could get out.

"Are you okay?" the person outside asked again.

She shook her head. "I don't know. Did you see that other car?"

"What other car?"

"The one that swerved in front of me. They pushed me into this one."

"Someone was in the crosswalk. They must have swerved to avoid them. Probably didn't even know you were there. They kept going."

"Dammit."

"Why don't you come over here and sit? My wife already called the police. They'll be here soon."

"The police?"

He nodded. "And an ambulance."

"Why?"

"Um, because you're bleeding."

Stacey looked down and saw blood on her shirt. She

reached up and felt the bite of pain when she touched her nose. "Ow."

"They'll be here soon to check on you. Is there anyone else you need to call? Your husband?"

The man gestured to the wedding rings Stacey never took off. Blood oozed around them on the inside, where the rings cut into her finger on impact.

"My purse is in the car."

"I'll get it for you. I'm Ricky. What's your name?"

"Stacey Allen."

"Nice to meet you Stacey. This is my wife, Molly."

"Hi," Stacey said.

"Hi. Are you okay? The police are on the way."

"Thanks. I'll be okay. I think."

Sirens echoed through the air. Stacey waited for Ricky to bring her purse back to her. She was about to call Wray when an ambulance pulled up in front with Station 37 on the side. Wray's house.

"Stacey? Are you okay?" Mark Andrews was on a different shift than Wray and Braden, but they all knew each other well. And their families.

"Hi, Mark. I've had better days. I was just about to call Wray when you guys pulled up."

"He's going to have a fit if he hears about this from anyone else. You better call him quick. Tell him we're going to take you to St. Nicholas."

Stacey nodded and dug out her phone. It rang three times before Wray answered, like he wasn't sure if he wanted to. "Yeah?"

"Hi, Wray. Um, it's me. I, uh, I got into an accident."

"What? Are you okay? Where are you? What happened?"

The rapid-fire questions were more comforting than the

disgruntled greeting. "I'm okay, but Mark is here. They're taking me to St. Nicholas. Can you meet me there?"

"Yeah. I'll be there soon."

"Okay, thanks. Bye."

"Hey, Stace?"

"Yeah?"

"Thanks for calling me."

"Thanks for answering."

He grunted something that sounded like agreement, then the line went dead.

"Let's get you loaded up. Is there anything else you need from the car?" Mark asked.

Stacey shook her head. "Ricky got my purse. I can get everything else another time."

"Can you stand?" Mark offered Stacey his hand and helped her to her feet. He didn't let go as she checked her balance and wobbled her way to the back of the ambulance.

The police were talking to Ricky and Molly and the others who'd come out of the nearby restaurant in the aftermath of the accident. A woman stared at the crumpled mess of the cars mashed together. She had to be the owner of the car Stacey plowed into.

The ambulance doors closed and the scene outside was cut off. Stacey felt guilty. She totaled her own vehicle and possibly the other woman's. She lost Oscar. And she had no new answers for Holly. She was letting everyone down.

Wray ran into the emergency department and went straight for the desk. He asked for Stacey and impatiently tapped his fingers on the counter that separated him from the person who was taking their sweet ass time figuring out where his wife was.

Finally, the woman looked up at him and said, "Bed nine."

"Thanks," Wray said, already turning and heading toward Stacey. The woman called after him, but Wray was not going to wait to be escorted. Not when he knew his way around the emergency department and needed to get to his wife.

Stacey was on a gurney with her eyes closed. Wray stepped to the side of the bed and looked her over. Bruising had already started on her face from the airbag. Her nose had a stere-strip over it, but it didn't look broken. She had another cut on her lip and a bruise on her forehead. Her clothes were spotted with blood, and her left ring-finger was wrapped up.

"It looks worse than it is," Stacey said softly.

"You're awake." Wray wanted to hold her tight and never let her go. She got hurt, and he wasn't there. It killed him to hear her voice on the phone and not be there with her. To worry that something worse than a few scrapes and bruises had marred her perfect body.

"I was just resting my eyes."

"Do you have a concussion?" Wray asked, staring at her eyes and studying them for dilation and focus. His medical training was better than most being a firefighter, but he only did quick assessments. Long-term care was not his wheelhouse.

"Probably, but minor, they think. I have to stay here for a few hours."

"Are they admitting you?"

"No."

"Then you can go home."

"They want to observe me."

"I can observe you. I'll talk to the doctor."

"Wray..."

Her tone stopped him before he made it out of the curtained area. She didn't want him to look after her. She'd rather stay in the hospital with strangers.

"I see," he said.

"You see what?"

"You don't want me to observe you."

She waited until he lifted his gaze to hers. "I was going to say thank you."

His brows tugged together. "You were?"

She nodded. "Yes. I don't like hospitals. You know that. I'd rather be home."

"Then I'll make it happen. I'll be right back."

"I'm not going anywhere."

He smiled at her, overwhelmed by the urge to kiss her. He took a step toward her and stopped. He didn't have the right to kiss her, but he couldn't stop himself. He shook his head and crossed the room to her side. He hugged her close and kissed the top of her head. "I'm so happy you're okay."

She hugged him back and nodded. "Me, too."

He stayed there another long minute, hating that his wife had to be hurt for him to touch her again, and hating himself for being grateful he could. He didn't want to let go, but he needed to get her out of there.

"I'll be back in a sec."

Stacey nodded, and Wray forced himself to walk out. He was putting her first, and that meant getting her the hell out of there. Now.

STACEY SETTLED on the couch at home, happy that she wasn't at the hospital any longer. Wray worked some magic to convince the doctor that he was capable and willing to watch her the way she needed to be to make sure she didn't suffer any permanent damage.

Wray brought her a water bottle and painkillers for her headache, handed her the remote, and fluffed the pillows around her so she was comfortable.

"Are you feeling okay? Do you need anything else?"

Stacey shook her head, grateful when it didn't hurt.

"Okay. I'm going to go pick up the boys if that's okay. Then I'm going to call into work and take a few days off. Have you spoken to Frannie?"

"I called her from the hospital before you got there."

"Okay, good. I can talk to Marcus, too. Make sure there's a complete investigation into the accident."

"It was my fault. I hit the other car."

"Someone swerved in front of you and pushed you into the car."

"I should have hit my brakes."

"Did they stop?"

Stacey shook her head and ducked her chin. She hadn't told Wray about Oscar. He knew she went to a funeral the weekend before, but he didn't know the situation. She didn't want to tell him. And explaining why she was following a random man through the city would bring up more questions than answers.

"Marcus needs to find that driver and ask why they didn't stop."

"He probably didn't see anything. The man who helped me said there were people in the crosswalk. The driver swerved to avoid them. There was nothing he could have done."

"Still. He should be questioned. He should have stopped to see if you were okay. He caused—"

"Wray," Stacey interrupted.

"Yeah?"

"Let it go. We'll figure out how to pay for it. Insurance should cover most of it. I'm sorry I got into an accident and put another strain on us financially."

"Stace, I'm not thinking about that at all," Wray said, moving closer to her. He crouched down in front of her. "I... You're hurt. And that kills me. I don't like to see you like this."

"I'll be fine. I feel better already. I promise."

Wray eyed her suspiciously.

Stacey pasted on her best fake grin and prayed he'd buy it. When he sighed and stood, she knew he was buying it enough to pretend he was buying it.

"Are you going to be okay while I get the boys?"

"Yes, I'll be fine."

"Don't get up or move around. Keep your phone with you, right in your reach. If you start to feel dizzy at all, call me." He stared at her until she nodded. He shook his head. "I'm just going to call Braden. He can be here in a minute and he can stay with you until I get home."

"I don't need a babysitter," Stacey protested.

Wray was already calling, ignoring her plea. "Hey, I need a favor. Stacey got into an accident. Yeah, she's okay, but I need to watch her for a concussion. She's home. That's the thing, I need to pick up the boys from school. Yeah? Really? Are you sure? Okay, thanks, man. See you soon."

"Is he coming to stay with me?" Stacey asked as Wray hung up the phone.

"No. He's going to pick up the boys so I can stay here with you."

"Really?"

Wray nodded. "He's on the pickup list. He's going to come by and grab my truck so he has carseats, but then he's going to get the boys. Is it okay if he stays for dinner? He can keep the boys busy so you can rest."

"Sure," Stacey said.

Wray looked up and nodded through the window to the front. "He's here. I'll be right back."

Stacey nodded. She didn't want to be in the hospital because she wanted peace, and now she was home and had even less. At least in the hospital, a nurse would have only checked on her every hour or so. If Wray wasn't willing to leave her alone to pick up the boys, she wasn't going to have a minute to herself.

He came back in and checked on her again, asking if she needed anything. Stacey assured him she was fine, then turned on the TV and tried to find something to take her mind off what happened.

She was sure Oscar saw her. He drove past her and gave her a look that said he was well aware it was her. Stacey tried to keep her distance when she followed him, but she couldn't help but wonder if Oscar knew she was there and created that accident to get her off his tail.

"How are you feeling? Is your headache better?" Wray asked.

Stacey had almost forgotten he was there. She wasn't watching the TV at all, just letting it play on the screen. "Um, I'm okay, I guess. Just thinking about work. Do you want to find something to watch? I'm not really focused."

"How's your headache?"

"It's okay. Still hurts."

"Does anything else hurt? Your neck or shoulder? Across your chest from the seatbelt?"

Stacey shook her head. "Not really."

"Good."

"The remote?" she offered again. If Wray got sucked into a show, he'd leave her alone for a little longer so she could think. She needed to find Oscar again, and prove he killed Holly. Preferably without getting killed herself.

Wray shook his head and told Stacey to put on whatever she wanted. She flipped the channel before stopping on a home renovation show. She set the remote down and stared blankly at the screen, letting her mind wander. She needed to get back to where they found Holly. If Oscar was there, there was a reason. Stacey needed to figure out what it was.

6

———

"Hey, you're here!" Frannie stopped on her way past Stacey's office and walked in. "I thought you'd take a day off. How are you?"

Stacey shook her head. "Frustrated."

"Why? The accident?"

Stacey looked up at her boss. She hadn't told anyone she was going to see where Holly died, and she definitely hadn't admitted she got into the accident because of Oscar. But Frannie would understand.

"I was following Oscar Hyatt."

"Holly's husband?" Frannie breathed.

Stacey nodded.

"That's why you got into the accident? Was it with him?"

"No. I was behind him, and he swerved, and to avoid hitting him, I swerved into a parked car. I was watching him and not really paying attention to everything else, but I don't know what else I could have done."

"Did he run you off the road?"

"Not technically. There was a husband and wife who

helped me. They said someone was in the crosswalk. That he had to swerve to avoid the people."

"Oh, my God. Stacey, you could have been killed."

"It was fine."

Frannie pursed her lips and gave Stacey a disapproving mom look. Then she sat down and relaxed. "I understand the desire to figure out what happened to Holly and to get Vera away from him, but you have to be careful."

"I didn't go out looking for him."

"Really? Because you said you were going to do exactly that after you got Holly's letter." Frannie's arched brow conveyed her disbelief.

"I went to where Holly's body was found. I just wanted to see the place. I don't really know what I was looking for, but I wanted to go there."

"And?"

"And Oscar drove by while I was there. He went slowly, then took off when I saw it was him."

"What?" Frannie breathed.

"It was weird. I mean, that area is pretty abandoned. I didn't think much of it when I heard the car approaching, but he was going really slow. Like he was watching me and knew it was me. I turned around and looked because I thought maybe someone needed directions or something, but he just smirked and took off."

"So, he definitely saw you?"

"No question."

"Wow. What was he driving? Did you get the license plate?"

"No, I didn't think to do that."

"What was he driving? We can look and see if it's regis-tered to him."

"It was a light blue sedan. Not very unique. It looked like

every other car out there."

"Do you know what kind of car?"

Stacey thought for a second and shook her head. "I'm not very good at this espionage thing."

"You'll get better. If he was down there, there's a chance it wasn't the first time. I know we believe he killed Holly, but driving down the same road does not prove anything. So, what's in that area? What could he have been doing there?"

Stacey shook her head. "Nothing seemed to be open. The warehouses were all pretty abandoned looking. No cars, no activity."

Frannie tapped her finger against her lip. "Sometimes people use abandoned warehouses to hide what they're doing. What does Oscar do for a living?"

"I have no idea."

"Let me see what information Marcus has about him." Frannie pulled out her phone and called Marcus.

Stacey tried not to eavesdrop on their conversation and busied herself with paperwork she intended to do the day before. She reviewed the file for Raina's discharge, noting the intended date was two weeks away. There was also a form requesting Karli Sloane attend a therapy session with Raina on Monday. Stacey signed it, happy Raina had found a safe place to live. Stacey would follow up with Raina after she left Shelter in the Storm, but after Holly, it was good to know another woman wouldn't be on her own and vulnerable to the monster who thought he could use her as a punching bag.

Frannie hung up and met Stacey's gaze. "Oscar doesn't drive a blue sedan. And he doesn't work or live anywhere near where you saw him."

"So, what was he doing there?"

Frannie shrugged. "I think we need to find out."

Oscar Hyatt walked into the warehouse with a grin on his face. He not only shook the bitch who was following him the day before, but he got her into an accident. He hadn't been able to stop smiling since.

She thought she was going to find something on him, but she was dead wrong. He was too smart to get caught. He'd proven that more than once over the years. And with the people he was working for, there was no way he'd get caught. They'd make sure of it.

"Did you make the delivery yesterday?" his boss, Damon, called out.

Oscar hurried to the office Damon used in the far corner. The rest of the warehouse was storage. Oscar wasn't sure exactly why there were so many car parts in there, but he supposed it didn't really matter as long as the work was getting done.

"Yeah, boss. All good."

"Did you run into any issues?"

Damon looked up at Oscar. The slice through his dark brow not moving with the lift of the rest of it. Oscar knew his boss was a badass, but he also knew Damon didn't get his hands dirty. That was Oscar's job. One he was more than happy to prove he was ready to move on from.

"All good," Oscar lied. He'd been on his way to the pickup when he spotted that shrink lady on the sidewalk. He thought about running her down, but it was too careless after he'd been driving the car around. He could torch it, but he didn't have time to take care of her, the car, and get his job done. She almost blew it for him when she followed him, but she got hers.

"Good. I'd like you to do another run for us. The shipment is coming in on Friday at ten pm. You need to meet the driver and take the product to the warehouse up north."

"What's the product?"

Damon glared at him. "Does it matter?"

Oscar shrugged. "Nah, man. Just curious."

"Do you know who's curious?"

Oscar shook his head.

"Dead men and cops. Which are you?"

Oscar's cheeks heated at the implication. He shuffled his feet and shook his head, hoping his boss didn't really think Oscar was a rat. He'd rather be dead than have someone think he would join the Company only to try to take them down.

"Neither, man. Neither."

"Then stop asking questions."

"Yep. Do you have an address for me to meet the driver?"

"I'll get it to you Friday by nine."

"Sounds good. You got anything for me to do between now and then?"

"No."

Oscar waited to see if Damon elaborated, but he didn't.

"Okay. Good. Well, I'll talk to you Friday."

Damon arched that eyebrow again, dismissing Oscar.

Oscar nodded and got the hell out of there. He wasn't afraid of Damon or anything, but Damon was a scary dude. You know, if someone was afraid. But Oscar definitely wasn't. Nah. Not at all.

STACEY SPENT the next few days looking into everything she could about Oscar. Because Vera was living with him, she had access to Vera's records, which included an address.

Stacey drove by the house a few times during the week, wondering if Vera was safe. She never saw either Vera or Oscar, but lights were on once it got dark outside and the mail appeared to be collected every day.

Stacey didn't like stalking someone, but Oscar was a dangerous man, and Stacey was not going to let him hurt Vera.

Late Friday night, Stacey decided to do one more drive-by to see if she could see anything. Next week, she planned to watch his work. Not that she expected to catch him doing something illegal out in the open, but she needed to get an idea of his routine.

Then maybe she could think about searching the house. Even thinking it was crazy, but Stacey couldn't get the idea out of her head that she would find something.

Stacey turned down Oscar's street just as a car left his driveway. Stacey's heart skipped. Her palms dampened on the steering wheel. Should she follow him? Or should she just go home like she planned?

She debated for five minutes as she followed a dark car, different from the other day, from a distance. It wasn't easy so late at night when her headlights announced her presence, but she hoped it was not as obvious as she felt.

Oscar turned into the parking lot for a big box store that was open twenty-four hours. He parked toward the back of the lot. Stacey parked closer to the front, where she could watch him, and turned off her car, watching for him to do the same.

She sat there for ten minutes, staring at his parked car. The engine was still running, and the lights were on. She debated getting out and going into the store to make it more credible that she ended up there, but he didn't seem to be paying any attention to her. He was staring at something in his lap.

His face glowed for a minute, then he lifted a phone to his ear. Stacey didn't know what it meant that he parked in a lot like this and waited for a phone call, but it was odd.

A minute later, Oscar pulled out of the lot again. Stacey waited a few seconds, then followed him.

She stayed a little farther back this time, not taking any chances at getting into an accident again. She was already driving a rental, and a second accident in a week would not go over well with her insurance company, or her wallet.

Oscar turned into a fast food place and got in line for the drive-thru. Stacey debated what to do. If she followed him, it would be harder to hide the fact that she was following him. But if she didn't, how did she explain her presence?

Stacey drove around and parked in one of the reserved parking spots. She opened an app on her phone and put in an order for a coffee and fries, hoping it would be done quickly. She paid and closed the app.

Stacey watched the cars go through the drive-thru one by one. It wasn't overly busy, but there was a steady line of vehicles. She watched for the car Oscar was driving and started to panic when he was the second to get his food.

She stared at her mirror and watched as Oscar smiled at the girl in the window and accepted a bag of food from her. He said something that made her laugh. She nodded, tilting her head to the side and biting her lip.

The girl couldn't have been much older than Vera. What a sleaze. He finally pulled away from the window with a wave. The girl stared after his car until he turned to the left and out of sight.

Shit. Stacey was still waiting for her order. She didn't

really care about the order, but she didn't want it to be obvious she was following Oscar.

She debated for a few seconds if she should stay and wait or just go. She was about to pull out when someone knocked on her window. The bag of food in her view prompted her to roll down her window.

Stacey started to reach for the bag when the person holding it snatched it away and slammed her arm back. Stacey called out as pain radiated down her arm.

"Why the fuck are you following me?"

"Oscar," Stacey breathed. It was all she could do to push his name out past the pain she felt.

"Yeah, and I know who you are, you fucking bitch. You have no right to follow me. And if you don't stop, you're going to end up like my ex-wife."

"Holly. You killed her. I know you did."

"Cops said I didn't."

"You son of a bitch. If you hurt Vera—"

"That's my daughter," he snapped. "She's mine. I've never laid a hand on her. You don't get to decide anything about her. You have no right to talk to her. I'll make sure you never see her, or anyone else again, if you don't back the fuck off."

"You killed Holly, and I'm going to prove it."

He pressed a knife to her throat, so tight Stacey couldn't swallow without it cutting into her skin. She felt the blood trickle down her neck. A tear fell from the corner of her eye. She didn't even see the knife in his hand before she felt the cold steel of it against her skin, and then it was too late to do anything about it.

"You're not going to prove a damn thing. Because I'm smarter than you are, and I'm not going down for anything. They'll never let it happen."

"Who?" Stacey rasped, risking a deeper cut to ask the question.

The blade was gone, but before she could breathe a sigh of relief, he punched her in the cheek. Pain splintered through her face and stole the breath from her lungs. By the time the tears cleared from her eyes, he was gone.

"Are you okay, ma'am?" someone asked from right outside her window.

Stacey jumped and nearly scrambled over the center console to get away from the voice.

"Whoa, I didn't mean to scare you. I have your order."

"Did you see that man?" she rasped.

"What man?" the kid with the food asked, turning away from Stacey to look around at the empty lot. All the vehicles were in the drive-thru line.

"The one who was just here?" The pain was sinking in deeper, echoing through her entire body like a poison.

"There wasn't anyone out here when I walked out. I'm sorry. Um, do you need to call someone?"

Stacey looked past him to the road that ran in front of the store. Dead quiet. Not a car in sight. Did he knock her out?

"I'm good. Thanks for bringing the order to me."

He handed over the bag and hurried away from her, looking back at her car when he got to the door. He could think she was crazy all he wanted, but Oscar was there. She knew he was.

She lifted her hand and touched her cheek. She'd never felt that kind of pain before. It stung her cheekbone and made her entire face hurt. She gently touched the cut on her neck, wincing at the thin line that oozed blood. Her arm hurt where he slammed it against the doorframe, but she could move it and didn't think it was broken.

But the way her vision was going blurry, she wasn't sure she should drive.

Stacey drew a breath, wincing when it made her face hurt. She grabbed her phone with her right hand, holding her left gingerly against her body. She called the only person she knew would come and not get upset about it.

"Frannie. I need help."

Ten minutes later, Frannie and Marcus pulled in. Marcus took one look at her face and declared he was taking her to the hospital.

"No," Stacey begged. "Please. Nothing's broken. The bruises will heal. But I can't go home like this. I'll scare the boys and Wray will lose it."

"He needs to know," Marcus growled.

"I'll tell him."

"Why didn't you call him to come get you?"

"Marcus!" Frannie said.

"What?"

"You're going to make her think we're upset she called. Stacey, we are always here for you."

"You know we are, Stace, but why didn't you call your husband? I'd be furious if this happened to Frannie and she didn't call me."

"If I called him, I'd have to tell him what I was doing. But not only that, he'd have to find someone to watch the boys and someone else to drive him here so we could bring my car home. That would mean getting more people up. Calling you two was easier."

"Except for the part about wondering what you're doing," Marcus said with his cop look.

Stacey didn't like when Marcus looked at her the way he was. Firm and unbending in a way that made an innocent person squirm. Stacey had no idea how criminals didn't spill their guts when face-to-face with that look from Marcus. She'd never be able to keep anything from him.

"I was following Oscar Hyatt."

"The abusive husband? Shit, Stacey. That's a bad idea."

"He killed Holly. Holly sent me a letter that said—"

"I know about the letter," Marcus said. "That letter isn't proof of anything."

"Oscar admitted to me that he killed Holly."

"He admitted it? He said he killed her?"

"Yes. I mean, basically. He said if I didn't stop following him, I was going to end up like Holly and that the cops couldn't prove he did it. And he said he's not going down for anything because 'they'd' never let that happen."

"They? Who's that?"

Stacey shrugged. "I don't know. Whoever he works for, I guess."

"He works for a shipping company," Marcus said.

"I know, but I don't think that's who he really works for."

"You watch too much TV," Marcus said.

"And your poker face isn't as good as you think it is," Stacey told him.

"All right, you two," Frannie interrupted. "I think we need to get Stacey home. And we need to get back."

Marcus nodded. He helped Stacey around to the passenger seat of her own car, then got back in his truck. Frannie got behind the wheel and backed Stacey's car out of the parking space and turned onto the road.

"Are you really okay?" Frannie asked.

Stacey shook her head. "That was scary. I thought he was going to really hurt me."

"He did hurt you. And it could have been worse. You're lucky, Stace. And I know you want to prove—"

"Don't," Stacey interrupted. "Don't tell me to stop."

"I wasn't going to tell you to stop. I was going to tell you to be more careful and that I want to help you. He killed Holly, and he's threatening you. We need to put him away."

Tears sprang to Stacey's eyes. She nodded. "Thanks."

Frannie parked Stacey's car behind the shelter in the employee lot. Marcus pulled in right behind them. The three of them went to the medical center inside, stocked with basic first aid supplies to patch up anyone who showed up looking like Stacey.

There wasn't much they could do for her already swelling face, but Stacey accepted the ice pack Marcus gave her and hoped it would be good enough by morning to cover the bruise and cut with makeup. Frannie put butterfly bandages on the cut on Stacey's neck after cleaning it with antibacterial soap. Her arm had a bruise from where she hit the doorframe, but it hurt the least of all her injuries.

They were heading to the car when Marcus cleared his throat. "I called Wray."

"You what?" Stacey and Frannie said together.

"I wanted him to know what happened."

"I was going to tell him," Stacey said.

"Maybe, but I wanted him to know how bad your injuries were. If you're anything like Frannie, you're going to downplay things so he doesn't worry about you. But he has a right to worry about you."

Stacey nodded. She wasn't sure if Marcus knew how bad things had been between Stacey and Wray. It didn't matter because he was only doing what he thought was best.

Marcus followed them once more, but Frannie didn't say anything on the second drive. She kept glancing over at Stacey and biting her lip, but by the time they got to Stacey's house, Frannie hadn't spoken.

Then Wray was there. He opened the door for Stacey

and crouched down in front of her, his eyes red and wet. He brushed his hand over her face and neck, then closed his eyes and slid his hands over her shoulders and grabbed her hands in his. "Are you okay?"

Stacey shrugged. She would heal, but at the moment, she was in a lot of pain. And seeing her husband so upset definitely twisted her up inside and made it all worse.

"Let's get you inside and to bed." Wray stood and helped Stacey out of the car.

He wrapped his arm around her waist and let her lean on him. It felt good to lean on him.

Frannie locked the car and handed Stacey's purse and keys to Wray. He thanked them both and confirmed with Marcus the extent of her injuries, including the punch that might have knocked her out for a minute or two.

Inside, Wray guided her straight upstairs and eased her onto the bed. Stacey was already fading, her concussion from earlier in the week still making her tired more quickly than usual. The punch she took probably only making that worse.

"I think I just want to go to bed," she said as Wray found pajamas for Stacey to wear.

"Good. You need to rest. I'll help you change... I mean, if you're okay with that."

Stacey nodded. "Thanks."

He sucked in a breath when he saw the bruise on her arm, but he didn't say anything. He was gentle with her, tender. When she was changed, he lifted her feet and helped her slide under the covers.

"Let me get you some painkillers before you go to sleep. You're going to feel even worse in the morning."

Stacey nodded and sat up. When he came back, she took the pills, then rolled over and was asleep in seconds.

7

—————

Wray watched Stacey as she fell asleep. It didn't take her long, something that was unusual for her. Stacey always worried about everyone else, and that worry kept her up most nights long after Wray fell asleep.

Having their roles reversed gave Wray a new sense of his wife. He always thought her worrying was silly, but sitting in the chair in the corner of their bedroom and watching her sleep was the only thing he could do. He couldn't get up and leave. He couldn't fall asleep himself. He couldn't do anything except watch her and convince himself she was safe.

When Marcus called, Wray's entire body went still. He was used to seeing people hurt, but his own wife? That was different. He paced in front of the window, waiting for Stacey to get home, and when he saw the cars pull up, he had to hold himself back from yelling at her. Not that he was angry, or at least not only angry, but he was scared out of his mind.

She could have been killed. She could have been hurt a lot worse than she was. He didn't know what she was doing or why she was at a fast food place so late at night, but none of that really mattered. What mattered was that she was home, and he wasn't going to let anything else happen to her.

As Wray sat there, he calmed his heartbeat and his body. Part of his training taught him to relax his body and mind during fires, but also so he could sleep whenever he had the chance to do so. Even though he was tense and worried, he forced himself to close his eyes and eventually, sleep came.

Wray bolted upright when he heard Stacey whimper. It took him a second to remember what happened the night before and why he was in the chair in their bedroom, but as soon as he did, his gaze snapped to Stacey. She was still asleep, stirring in her sleep. Her face twisted with the pain she felt, then she groaned. Her hand went to her bruised cheek, and a sigh shook her entire body.

"Ow," she said out loud.

"It'll be sore for a while," Wray said, knowing she was awake even if her eyes weren't open.

Her gaze found his, then scanned his position in the chair next to the bed. "Did you sleep there?"

Wray nodded. "How are you feeling?"

"Like I got my ass kicked."

"I'm sorry. I'll get you some painkillers. Hopefully they help." Wray got up and retrieved the pills from the bathroom. He filled Stacey's cup with water and carried both back to her.

She was sitting up in bed, her pajamas concealing the bruises on her arm but not the ones on her neck and face.

Wray paused, needing a breath so he didn't lose it. The butterfly bandages on her throat held together a thin cut that stretched almost three inches across her skin. The bruising on her face was black and blue and covered her entire cheek. Wray could barely stand to see the wounds. But how he felt didn't matter.

"Thanks," Stacey said when Wray handed her the pills and water. She swallowed them down, then handed the cup back to him. "You didn't have to sleep here."

"I couldn't leave you. I'm sorry. I know you don't want me here, but when you got home last night... I couldn't leave you."

"It's okay," Stacey said, her lips curling up into a tentative smile. "I appreciate it."

"I haven't heard the boys yet. Do you want to shower before they get up?"

Her gaze strayed to the bedroom door, and her hand went to her neck. "I should, but I'm not sure what to do about the bandages."

"It's probably best to leave those on for now, and we can change them when you get out. I can clean it for you and make sure it's okay. If you want."

Stacey nodded. "Thank you."

Wray smiled at her. She wasn't pushing him away, which was a nice change over the last few months. He was sure she was just scared and overwhelmed, but maybe it was something more than that.

Stacey eased the covers back and set her feet on the floor. She pushed to stand and wobbled a bit. Wray stepped forward to help, holding the arm that wasn't bruised. Together, they walked to the bathroom, with Stacey leaning on Wray.

He turned the shower on for her, then asked if she needed help with anything else. She bit her lip. "Will you help me get in?"

Wray swallowed and nodded. He hadn't seen his wife completely naked in more than six months. Even when he changed her last night, she kept her bra and panties on. But now, she was getting in the shower.

Wray hooked his thumbs in the waistband of her shorts and panties, easing both down her legs. The room filled with steam, adding to the heat that pulsed through his entire body. He could smell her unique scent, the one he called up when he showered and jerked off, thinking about his wife and getting another chance with her.

Stacey put her hands on his shoulders and stepped out of the bottoms one foot at a time. Wray moved them to the side so she didn't trip, then stood. Stacey kept her hands on his shoulders and looked up at him through her lashes in a way she hadn't looked at him in forever.

"Stacey," Wray groaned. He was hard and horny and wanted her so badly he could taste it, but he was not going to make a move on his wife.

"Yeah?"

"Your shirt?" He grabbed the hem and started to lift it. He was careful not to touch her skin unless he had to. He guided her uninjured arm through the sleeve, then eased the shirt up and over her head and slid it off her bruised arm without needing to lift that one.

Stacey met his gaze again, her lip locked between her teeth.

If Wray wasn't a fool, he would have thought Stacey was looking at him like she wanted him. He wanted to believe that, but it had only been five days since she asked him to move out. He couldn't take the chance.

"Can you get your bra, or do you need help?"

"I think I need some help. Please."

Wray nodded and swallowed thickly. He stepped forward and stared over Stacey's shoulder as he reached around her body. His hands easily found the clasp, but he fumbled to unhook it. Her hair tickled his nose and her warmth soaked into him. Having his arms around her made him impossibly harder and almost unable to hold himself back from pressing his body to hers.

The clasp mercilessly held, forcing him to stay close to her for several long seconds while he struggled to do something he'd done more time than he could count. When it finally released, the breath he didn't realize he was holding burst out of him in relief.

He stepped back as the bra slipped from her shoulders. Stacey tugged the strap off her sore arm and pulled it free from her full breasts.

Wray told himself not to look, but he was no saint, and his wife's breasts were works of art. He'd spent many nights worshipping them. Being so close to them as they swung free and unable to touch was painful for him.

Stacey took a step closer to him, forcing him to lift his gaze. She took another step, then lifted on her toes and pressed her lips to his.

The shock of it left Wray frozen in place. His hands hung at his sides, useless to grab hold of her and never let go. By the time his brain kicked in and screamed at the rest of him to react, she was stepping back again.

"Thanks for your help." A flush rose on her cheeks and settled to her breasts. She turned and stepped into the shower, closing the door and disappearing behind the steam covered glass.

Wray stumbled out of the room and wondered what the hell just happened. And how he could make it happen again.

WRAY SPENT the rest of the day with his family, wishing he wasn't on duty the following day. Their day was normal, like days used to be before he fucked up their family. Joey spent an hour at his friend's, but the rest of the time they were all together. And the boys didn't notice Stacey's injuries thanks to the turtleneck and expertly layered makeup she wore.

That night, Stacey sat on the couch with Wray and watched TV for a little while after the boys went to sleep. When she started to fade, she said good night, but it almost seemed reluctant. Wray asked if she needed help getting ready for bed, and she agreed.

He followed her up the stairs and into their bedroom. He closed the door so their voices didn't wake the boys. Stacey got clean pajamas from her drawer and laid them on the bed. She kicked off her slippers and sat on the edge of the bed to change her pants. When she was done, she stood in front of Wray with a vulnerable look in her eyes.

"Are you feeling any better tonight?" he asked softly.

"Some. My arm hurts a lot more today. My neck, too. I thought the turtleneck was a good idea, but it kept tugging on the bandages."

"You could have told me. I could have put something over them."

She shrugged. "There wasn't an easy way to get away from the boys."

"We would have figured it out. I'm sorry you're in pain. How's your cheek?"

"It's okay. Sore, but since I don't move it much, it's okay."

"Do you want to take your makeup off before or after you change your shirt?"

"After. It'll be easier without the turtleneck."

"Ready?" Wray asked.

Stacey nodded.

Wray held the sleeve so she could get her good arm out, then held the shirt away from her body to help her move that arm underneath. He lifted and stretched it over her head just like that morning, moving the shirt away from her face and neck, then guided it down her arm, doing his best to avoid touching where she was hurt.

Her bra was simple and familiar, but it was still on his wife. Most of the time she slept without one, but Wray didn't know what she intended to do.

"On or off?"

"Off, please. If that's okay."

Wray nodded and moved behind Stacey. Her back was entirely bare except for the band and straps that stretched across her skin. He wanted to lick his way up and down her spine and bend her over and have his way with her, but he still wasn't allowed to touch her.

He unhooked her bra with ease this time, his shaking hands more easily controlled when he could see what he was doing. He separated the band and pushed the straps off her shoulders.

She took a step back, resting her back against his front. His hands were on her shoulders. She let her bra fall to the floor, giving him a top view of her bare breasts.

His cock pulsed against her ass, begging to be let in. His fingers tightened on her shoulders, dying to cup her breasts. It was torture to be so close to her, to have his hands on her, and not be able to do anything.

"Stacey," he groaned softly.

"I miss you," she admitted.

"I miss you, too, Stace. So much."

She turned in his arms and wrapped her arms around his neck, pressing herself up and closer to him. His brain got the message this time, and he was fully engaged.

Wray's hands cupped her hips, drawing her body tight against his. When her lips met his, he was an eager participant in the tender kiss that sent lightning through his body. She parted her lips and tentatively darted inside his mouth with her tongue. He stroked his alongside hers, loving the taste of her in his mouth.

Wray didn't know where this was going, so he didn't push. He just held his wife and kissed her, pouring everything into the kiss so she knew he was there and always would be if she wanted him.

Stacey pulled back a minute later, gentling the kiss before resting her head on Wray's chest. They both breathed heavily, their bodies shaking. He held her, unsure what happened but loving every second.

"I'm sorry," she whispered.

Wray leaned back and lifted her chin so she would meet his gaze. "I'm not. I love you. I still want you. And you can kiss me any time you want. Or anything else, Stace. I'm always going to be yours."

She nodded, then reached for her shirt. Wray helped her guide it on, then kissed her cheek and walked out of the bedroom.

He'd take what he could get and not push for more. And he'd enjoy the hell out of it.

OSCAR RETURNED to the warehouse first thing Monday morning. He didn't hear anything from Damon all weekend, so he kept quiet and spent some time with Vera. Took her shopping. She was happy. Women were easy to please if you threw enough cash at them, and after the drop Oscar did Friday night, he was flush.

Damon's voice could be heard clear across the warehouse when Oscar walked in. The entire building was soundproof, but Damon had no problem letting anyone who walked inside know exactly what he thought of them. Someone was getting their ass handed to them.

Oscar waited outside the office, ignoring the guards who stood in front of Damon's door. They didn't let anyone in without Damon's permission. The guns and knives they wore in full display said they weren't interested in a pissing match. They'd cut or shoot someone without a second thought if they thought there was a reason for it.

"Is Oscar here yet?" Damon barked through the door.

The guy on the right took a step to the side and opened the door, stepping back for Oscar to walk through. Oscar nodded at him, then faced his boss, wondering why Damon didn't look happier.

"I heard you were late to meet the driver on Friday night. I don't accept tardiness."

"I was being followed," Oscar hurried to say. "I didn't want her to follow me all the way to the meet. I stopped by a drive thru."

"And you lost her?"

"She decided it was in her best interest not to follow me."

"What does that mean?" Damon growled.

Oscar's smirk melted away. He shuffled his feet. "I made sure she knew following me was a bad idea. She doesn't know anything about the Company. She thinks I killed my wife."

"Did you?"

"Yeah, but there's no proof. I made sure of it."

"The cops don't always need proof in order to put you away."

"Nah, I was cleared. Had an alibi and everything."

"How do you have an alibi?"

"A friend helped me out. Swore we were out together. Got a bunch of people to say we were at a restaurant."

Damon arched his eyebrow, glaring at Oscar until he blurted out everything.

"My bitch of a wife took my kid and left. She went to this shelter and I couldn't find her, but she got out a month ago. I found out where she was and where she was living and cornered her. Took her out in the middle of the day. No cameras, no witnesses, just me and her."

"And all the people who swore they saw you."

"They don't know shit."

"Are you really that stupid? A good alibi is one that can't be disproven. With how many people you have saying they saw you, all it takes is one of them to flip and say they were paid or they were lying or whatever, and you're done."

"They won't."

"And you know this for sure? Why would they lie for you?"

"I'd do the same. They know it."

Damon rolled his eyes like he didn't trust Oscar, but Oscar knew his buddies wouldn't let him down. He could trust them. They'd never sell him out.

"So, back to the woman who's following you. Why?"

"She thinks I killed my wife."

"Which you did."

"Yeah, but she doesn't know that. She works at the shelter. She was a counselor or something. She convinced Holly to stay away from me. To start a new life and move on without me. Holly was my fucking wife. She had my damn kid. That fucking bitch had no right to convince them to leave me. She should have been talking Holly into keeping our family together."

"Who's this woman?"

"Who?"

"The one who's following you. Do you know her name and where she works?"

"Stacey Allen. She works at Shelter in the Storm. Stupid name. Fucking place. But don't worry. I made sure she knows not to follow me again. And the delivery was all good. I got there less than ten minutes late, and the driver was all good. It's no big deal."

"No big deal," Damon repeated.

"Yeah, man. All good. So, you got anything else for me?"

Damon nodded. "Yep. I sure do."

8

Stacey had a full day on Monday. After her weekend recovering from Oscar, she was even more determined to not only prove he killed Holly, but to help the others staying at Shelter in the Storm to be safe after they left. Frannie created a place where women could escape the evil men they fell in love with, and helping them was more than a job for Stacey, but letting them down and having them end up like Holly was worse than a failure. It meant a woman who should have been around to share her light with the world was gone because of a selfish, evil man.

Stacey was not going to let it happen again.

Her first few sessions went as planned. One woman was brand new, a resident as of that weekend. It was Stacey's first time meeting her, and the woman was scared and uneasy. The more they talked, the more she relaxed, but she was having a hard time imagining a life after Shelter. Stacey hoped that would change over time.

The next appointment was with a woman who'd been staying at the shelter for a few months. She was single and had no one in the area to support her, so she was looking to start over somewhere else. Leave Niagara Falls and create a new life for herself. A life she seemed very excited about. Stacey was happy for her and enjoyed helping her plan the next part of her life, with tools to stay safe and healthy.

Stacey's third appointment was Raina. She brought her friend, Karli, to the appointment. Karli was a tall Black woman with springy curls and a friendly, welcoming smile. Stacey liked her on sight.

"It's so nice to meet you," Karli said, shaking Stacey's hand eagerly. "I think we have another friend in common."

Stacey tilted her head, unsure who Karli was talking about. She didn't look familiar. "Really?"

"Do you know Jessica German?"

Stacey laughed. "I do. Her boss's brother is my husband's best friend. We all get together sometimes. Taylor loves throwing parties and having everyone in her world over."

"That's what Jess told me. She speaks highly of you and Wray. When Raina told me we were coming here to meet with you, I wondered if there could be another Stacey Allen who's a social worker in Niagara Falls at a shelter."

Stacey liked Karli, and having the connection to Jessica made her that much more confident Raina would be safe with her. That was the most important part of the meeting. And making sure Karli knew she could come to Stacey if she ever had a concern. "I guess it's possible. Tell me how you two know each other."

Karli looked at Raina to let her answer. Stacey appreciated that Karli wasn't trying to take over and respected that Raina needed to speak for herself.

"We went to college together. We lived across the hall from each other our freshman year and kept running into each other in the common kitchen area late at night when we were studying. We started chatting and just became friends. After our freshman year, we roomed together the rest of college." Raina smiled at Karli.

"Have you been in touch lately?" Stacey asked. Old friends were usually the first people exes contacted when they were trying to find their estranged partners. They could both be at risk if Raina's ex knew she was moving in with Karli.

"No, we haven't," Raina answered. "I moved here after graduation for my job, but Karli was on the West Coast. She just moved back to the area recently."

"I was working in LA, but the lifestyle wasn't worth it for me. I wanted to be a full-time artist, but I needed to have a job to support myself before that happened, so I got my masters in art therapy and started working. I love it, and after a while, I gave up the idea of being a full-time artist and decided to do it for fun, but then staying in LA no longer felt like the right thing to do." Karli shrugged like it was a logical choice, but Stacey needed more information.

"Where are you from?"

"I grew up in Cleveland. Jessica and I grew up together. Raina and I went to college in Dayton, Ohio. After that, I went to LA. My family is scattered throughout the country, and I was never really close to my brothers. My parents have a camper that they live in. I didn't really have roots anywhere, which was part of what I didn't love about LA. I didn't have people I connected with. Friends I could count on. I got sick a year ago and there was no one to even run to the store and pick up soup for me. It hit home that I wasn't really living my life, just existing, and I wanted a change. Jessica talked a lot about living here, and the city atmosphere plus the more relaxed feel appealed to me. It took me a few months, but I moved here over the summer.

Right after she was attacked. It was only after I moved here that I realized Raina lived here, too."

Karli maintained eye contact as she spoke. She glanced at Raina occasionally, but she didn't shift her gaze or look like she was hiding anything. Stacey trusted her.

"You know why Raina's here?" Stacey asked.

Raina leaned forward. "I told her everything. I thought about leaving, but part of why I got so sucked into Damon's world was because I didn't have anyone. I'm not sure he knows who Karli is. I might have mentioned her once or twice, but not regularly."

"You feel like you'll be safe with Karli?" Stacey asked directly, not leaving any room for misinterpretation. She needed the answer, and she needed to know Raina was answering that exact question.

"I do. I think we both need someone in our lives, and we're going to get together with Jessica, too. We all need friends."

Stacey nodded. She didn't want to admit she was a little jealous of the women. Stacey didn't have friends. She loved Taylor, but Stacey only knew Taylor because she was Braden's sister. If Stacey and Wray split up for good, Taylor would be on Wray's side with her brother. Stacey had Frannie, but Frannie was also her boss.

"I think having friends to lean on is always a good thing. You're all lucky to have each other."

Karli and Raina shared a smile. "Thanks."

The rest of the session went well. Raina was feeling good and happy. She was worried about her ex finding her, but she was hopeful he'd moved on to someone else in the time she'd been in the shelter.

When Raina and Karli left her office, Stacey checked her phone. She had one missed call from a blocked number, but the person didn't leave a message. A lot of former guests got disposable phones or prepaid phones to make them harder to find. Stacey worried whoever called was someone who needed help.

Stacey had lunch and was settling back in her office to catch up on paperwork when her phone rang. It was a blocked number again.

"Hello, this is Stacey."

"You need to stop interfering in other people's lives," said an angry man on the other end of the phone.

"Excuse me?" Stacey tried to place the voice.

"Don't play dumb with me, you bitch. I know everything about you, Mrs. Allen. I know where you live. I know all about your two sons. And I know you told your husband he needs to move out."

"Who is this?" Stacey breathed.

"It's a concerned citizen. You need to back off on your investigation."

"What investigation?"

"You know what I'm talking about. But if you're not sure, keep pushing. Maybe I'll pay a visit to your family. I think it's your husband's turn to pick your boys up today, isn't it? I'd hate for anything to happen to them."

Stacey opened her mouth to reply, but the man had already hung up. Her hands shook as she set the phone on her desk. She knew Frannie had been threatened many times, but it had never happened to her.

Stacey didn't know what to do. The only person she could think of who would call her was Oscar. And if he was, it had to mean she was getting close to finding something. He wouldn't go to that extent if there was nothing for her to find. But she couldn't risk her family getting hurt. Her boys and Wray.

They were the most important things in her life. Even being hurt and upset with Wray, she loved him. She couldn't let anything happen to him. Not now, not ever.

WRAY WAS STANDING in front of his closet when the phone rang. It had been a week since Stacey asked him to leave. After their weekend, he wanted to believe things were better, but she hadn't said she changed her mind and wanted him to stay. He told himself he should be packing, but he hadn't been able to bring himself to do it yet. He decided the interruption was a sign.

Especially when he saw it was Stacey.

"Hey," he answered, hoping he sounded casual. He felt strangely guilty being in their bedroom, and even more when he was thinking about packing up his stuff.

"Wray?" she asked. Her voice trembled. He went on high alert.

"Stace. What's wrong? Are you okay? The boys?"

"I'm...the boys are fine. I just... I just got a weird phone call. Did you tell anyone that I asked you to move out?"

He paused. What the hell kind of question was that? "I talked to Braden about it last week. He asked how things were going. Why? Did he say something to you?"

"No, it wasn't Braden."

"Okay, what happened? Who called you?"

She breathed a heavy sigh that shuddered through the phone. "I don't know who it was. He threatened me. He said something about you and the boys, too. He knew you were picking the boys up today. Said he hopes nothing happens to you."

"He threatened you?" Wray asked. Every inch of his

body tightened with rage. He sucked as a husband, but he was not going to let anything happen to his family.

"Frannie gets threats, and usually it's nothing, but this... I've never gotten a call like this."

"Do you know who it was?"

"I have an idea. Or at least what they were talking about."

"Do you think it's someone who'd actually do something? Who'd come after you or the boys?"

Stacey exhaled a long breath. He could picture her with her head in her hands, staring at the wall. Stacey was the calmest person he knew. She was patient and balanced and unbelievable. But when something shook her, it was hard for her to bounce back from it.

"I don't know. He's dangerous, I know that. I don't know what he would do."

"Did you call Marcus?"

"Not yet, but I will."

"Good. Hopefully he can help. What do you want me to do? Should I call school and tell them to make sure no one gets the boys who isn't on the list? I can walk in and get Joey instead of letting him go through the line."

"No, I don't want to scare the boys. I just... Did you make plans to move out yet?"

Wray hesitated. He hadn't, but the subject change threw him. Braden offered to let him stay, and Wray'd been debating it, but nothing was settled yet.

"I just... I don't feel safe without you there. I know it's a lot to ask, but can you stay? Just until we figure this out?"

Wray nodded, feeling grateful for a little more time. Maybe nothing would change, but maybe it was a second chance. "Of course. I'll stay as long as you want me to."

"Thank you. I don't want to take any chances that something happens to the boys. If he knows where we live, then he could be even more dangerous than I thought."

"Do you want me to come get you?"

"No. I'll be fine. Just make sure you're not late to get the boys today."

"I won't be. Hey, Stace?"

"Yeah?"

"I'm sorry...this happened to you."

"Thanks," she said weakly. "I'll talk to you soon. I need to go."

"Yeah, okay. Talk soon."

Stacey hung up, and Wray kicked himself. He wanted to tell her he was sorry for everything else that had happened. He already apologized more than once, but he felt like he needed to say it again. But apologizing for being an ass felt wrong when she was worried for their safety.

Wray looked back at his clothes in the closet and promised himself he would finally fix things with Stacey and never have to think about moving out again.

STACEY WAS on edge until she walked in her front door and saw Wray and the boys. Her lip wobbled, and she nearly lost her battle against her tears, but she held it together.

Wray looked up at her with a knowing look in his eye. He smiled and walked over, wrapping her up tight in his arms. "Nothing to report from their days," he whispered into her hair.

"Thank you," she breathed, barely pushing the words out. She felt better just having him there, his arms around her and their sons laughing and playing a few feet away. She'd missed him so much, and even though things weren't okay between them, it felt good to have him there. To rely on him.

"I fixed dinner. It's in the oven. It was on the menu for the week, so hopefully I did the right thing. And I have a bottle of wine in the fridge for you."

Stacey laughed. "It's been a long time since I've had a bottle of wine."

Wray chuckled, the rumble vibrating through her body. "You don't have to drink the whole bottle, but if you want to, I'm not going to stop you."

Stacey shook her head. "Just one glass sounds good right now." She kept her arms around him for another long moment, reluctant to let go even though she was desperate to change out of her work clothes.

"Do you want to get changed before dinner? It should be ready in about ten minutes," Wray said as if he was reading her mind.

Stacey nodded and finally stepped back, already missing the feel of his arms. "Thanks for being here."

"There's nowhere else I'd rather be," he said.

She smiled and nodded. There's nowhere else she'd rather he was, either. That truth sank in as she walked up the stairs and changed into sweats and a tank top. The thin fabric brushed over her nipples and tightened them. It had been far too long since sex was an option, and after the last week, Stacey was really wishing she could lose herself in her husband for a while.

Brushing the idea aside as unfair to both of them, Stacey added a sweatshirt to her outfit and went back downstairs. The boys were still deep in their game, so Stacey went to the kitchen and poured herself a glass of wine. She leaned against the counter and took a sip. It was one of her favorites, and it was perfect after the stress of the day.

Wray and the boys came into the kitchen a few minutes later. Stacey helped get dinner served and asked the boys how their days were.

"We had to do spelling words today," Joey said with a scowl. "I don't like spelling."

"Did you know the words?" Stacey asked.

"Yeah, but tests are dumb. I wanted to just tell the teacher the answer, but I got in trouble when I did that."

Stacey snorted. "You can't do that during a spelling test."

"Why not?"

"Because then the other kids will hear. They need to know how to spell the words, too."

"Yeah, but if I tell them, then they know. Why is that bad?"

Stacey and Wray shared a smile and shook their heads. It was tough having a kid who was crafty and clever and quick.

Evan's day was less exciting. He didn't have any tests. His class was learning colors and numbers. Evan declared his new favorite color was green.

"That's my favorite. You can't have the same favorite as me," Joey argued.

"Why not?" Wray asked. "My favorite color is blue, and that's Braden's favorite color, too."

"Yeah, but Evan's copying me," Joey stated.

"How do you know that?" Stacey asked.

"Because he always does. He likes red. He doesn't like green."

"I like gween!" Even shouted.

Joey rolled his eyes, and Stacey gave him a look that said he needed to knock it off. "I think there's enough green for both of you. And you don't need to get upset if your brother likes things you like. You might like a dark green and he likes a yellow-green, or maybe he likes green with more blue in it. Even if you like the exact same green, it's not like he's hurting you by liking the same thing."

"It's still dumb."

Stacey rolled her eyes and wondered if she'd ever be able to understand boys.

After dinner, they all sat in the living room and watched the newest superhero movie. Being the one and only girl in a house of boys meant Stacey had to learn to love the things they loved. She was not going to ever complain about watching hot men save the world. This was one of the things she didn't have to pretend to enjoy.

Evan was falling asleep when the movie ended, so Wray carried him upstairs to his bed after he said goodnight to Stacey. Joey said goodnight to her, too, leaving Stacey in the living room alone when the three of them went upstairs.

She double checked the locks and made sure all the curtains were closed tight. She listened as Wray read the boys a quick story and made her way upstairs while he was still talking.

She was sitting on the edge of the bed when he finished the book and said goodnight. He walked into the bedroom and stopped, surprised she was there.

"Sorry. I didn't mean to intrude."

"It's okay. I just didn't want to be downstairs alone."

"Are you doing okay?"

She shrugged. "It's hard thinking someone might want to hurt you or the boys because I'm trying to help someone in his life."

"Not everyone can think rationally about the people in their lives. If they could, they probably wouldn't have done something to send the women to Shelter in the Storm in the first place."

"Very true."

"Did you talk to Marcus today?"

Stacey nodded. "Why don't you close the door so we don't wake up the boys?"

Wray hesitated, then did as she suggested. He looked around the room like he wasn't sure what to do inside with her. Less than a year ago, he would have been on his side of the bed and had her curl up against his side and tell him everything.

She wanted that again. She wanted her husband back. She wanted things to be normal and good between them. Even if it was only for one night.

"Wray?" she said softly, looking up at him.

He swallowed audibly. "Yeah?" The word came out like a breath.

"Will you make me forget today? Please? Just for tonight."

His eyes darkened and blazed into hers. His jaw tightened. She would beg if she needed to, but she really hoped she wouldn't have to because the only thing she wanted in that moment was to feel her husband's body move with hers.

She prayed he wanted the same.

9

———————

Wray was not a fool. He knew it would kill him in the morning if she pretended nothing happened and if things went back to the way they were, but he would regret it for the rest of his life if he rejected his wife and never had another chance to be with her. How he felt didn't matter in that moment. All that mattered was Stacey.

He took a step toward her, watching her face as she realized he was agreeing. Relief sagged her shoulders and eased her entire body. When he stepped into her personal space, she eased her hands up his chest and around his neck, tilting her head to accept his kiss.

Being together was as natural as breathing. She knew his moves, and he knew hers. It was familiar and comfortable and everything sex should be with the person you love. Wray didn't have to think about how to make Stacey feel good because he knew her inside and out. He knew what she liked and what she loved. But after so many months apart, he felt like she was new to him again. Familiar but not. Comfortable but not. She was his wife...but not.

She parted her lips under his and pressed her tongue to

the seam of his mouth. He opened for her, eager to let her in. He was not going to rush the night. He needed it to last, to drag out her pleasure as long as possible. If she wanted to forget, he was going to make sure she forgot everything outside of the two of them in that moment. Their messy past and uncertain future were replaced by one night of a perfect present.

Wray cupped her neck and brushed his thumb along the edge of her jaw. She trembled against him, moaning softly. He glided his tongue next to hers, a slow, lazy stroke intent on learning her all over again. Stacey pressed her body to his, but he didn't speed things up. He was going to extend her pleasure and make sure he delivered exactly what she asked for.

Stacey stopped pushing after a minute and sank into the kiss. Wray could feel the shift in her. She wasn't trying to fight him or rush. She was enjoying the moment. She let her hands slide from around his neck. She touched his chest, lingering over his muscles in apparent appreciation for the work he did to stay in good shape. She traced his pecs, then scratched her nails over his nipples.

He groaned, hardening with each touch. His hand slid down her back to her ass, hauling her body against his. She squeaked with the sudden move, then melted into him. They were both fully clothed, but that only made the entire thing more erotic for Wray. He knew what was coming. And he was torturing himself as much as Stacey with the antic-ipation.

Wray finally moved them toward the bed, but he still didn't tug at her clothes or his. He sat on the edge and drew her down on top of him, straddling his hips with her knees on the mattress. She moaned when her center met his erec-tion and rubbed against him. He doubted his choice for a moment as his hormones screamed at him to flip her and fuck her, but he held back.

Sex with Stacey was an event, especially sex after months apart, and he was not willing to miss any of it. He slid his hands up her back, drawing her sweatshirt up and off her body. He left her tank top on, but he pulled back to see the way her hard nipples pressed to the thin fabric.

He leaned down, capturing one nipple through the cotton. He bit the tight peak and sucked it into his mouth, soaking her shirt. She writhed on his lap, rubbing herself against him and moaning as he teased her. He let go and bit down harder on the other nipple, handling her a little rougher as she rode him.

Stacey grabbed the edge of her tank top and yanked it over her head. She tossed it behind her, then offered her breasts to him, lifting them with her hands to his eager mouth.

Wray alternated between them, sucking and biting and loving them until her hips rocking nearly had him losing control of the tentative hold he had on his erection. It had been far too long since he'd had his hands and mouth and cock on his wife, and the last thing he wanted to do was blow his load in his pants before he ever got to feel her come.

"Oh, God," she moaned, her hips shifting faster as she raced toward the peak.

Wray flipped them, removing his pulsing cock from between her thighs. He ripped her sweatpants off and pushed her thighs wide, then sucked hard on her clit, feeling her come on his tongue.

"Oh, God, Wray," she whimpered. "So good. So, so good."

She kicked her pants off her feet as she came down, but

he wasn't done with her yet. He licked her gently, giving her time to breathe, then pressed one thick finger into her.

She moaned long and loud, her body sucking his finger in deeper. He retreated and added a second finger, pumping them in and out of her tight channel while she adjusted to him.

"I've missed you," she whispered.

Wray looked up at her, catching her gaze. "I've always been right here, Stace. I always will be."

She nodded slightly, but the look in her eyes said that was the wrong answer. Shutters fell and the vacant look he'd seen far too much in the last few months started to filter in.

Wray wasn't going to let that happen. He wasn't going to lose her before he even had her. If this was his one and only night with her, he was going to make sure she remembered it forever, and not for all the wrong reasons.

Before she had a chance to pull back, he slammed his fingers deep into her. She tensed and moaned, her body in charge again. Wray withdrew, then slammed into her again, bringing his lips down to her clit while he fucked her hard with his fingers.

She panted and shook with the merciless way he treated her. She didn't always like to admit she liked it hard, but he knew she did. She told him one night, when they were sharing secrets and getting to know each other, and he'd never forgotten. It sent her mind spinning into space and her body left to run the ship. And her body only had one goal in mind when he fucked her hard. To come...hard.

Wray waited, knowing her body would tell him when she was close. His arm ached, but he kept going, licking her clit until she finally tightened around him. She tensed, every inch of her going rigid. He increased his pace and sucked hard on her clit, and she went flying.

She buried her face in a pillow and moaned into it. Her body gyrated all across the bed, chasing him and running away from him at the same time. He didn't let her come down from one orgasm before he was sending her right back up toward another. And when she was almost there, he pulled back and replaced his fingers with his cock. He grabbed her hips and crashed their bodies together, giving and taking, need and want and desire and love all mixed up together as they went flying together.

Wray's vision went black, his focus gone as he came with such force he thought he might pass out. His fingers indented the flesh at Stacey's hips. She pulsed around him, the aftershocks of her orgasms drawing him in and vibrating through his body.

He stared at her as he came back down to earth. Everything was Stacey. The way he felt, the way he came, the love inside him. It was all her. And the way she looked up at him with a sex-drunk happiness on her face told him he'd remember the moment forever.

He refused to think of it as a goodbye. He couldn't think of it as a new beginning, either. But he wanted to believe maybe it was something more than just one night. He'd loved her for years, and he wasn't ready to walk away from that. No matter how much he knew he fucked up and created the mess they were in, he knew he needed her. Not only that, but he wanted her. He wanted her to be his wife again, in every sense of the word. And he wasn't going to sit back and hope she would agree. He was going to fight.

Stacey smiled up at him, reaching for him to lean down and kiss her. He gave her a quick kiss, knowing she didn't love him to deepen it when she could taste herself on his lips. He wanted to say he loved her, but the best option was to stay quiet and let her lead. For now. Tomorrow, he would start to fight for his family.

Wray went to the bathroom and cleaned himself up. Stacey joined him after a minute, using the bathroom like it was any normal night for them. Wray took his time, letting her go back to bed first.

When he walked out, she was in bed with the covers pulled back on his side. Her shoulders were bare, her discarded clothes still on the floor.

"Do you want me to stay?" he asked softly, his voice catching with hope.

"You don't have to if you don't want to." Her tone had the same uneasiness he felt in his gut, and he knew it was hard for her to open the door for him.

He didn't answer, just moved to his side of the bed and got in. She turned toward him and curled against his side. He wrapped an arm around her and held her close, more determined than ever to never let go again.

STACEY WAS WONDERFULLY, happily sore the next morning. Wray was stoically passionate the night before, not once, but three times. She couldn't remember the last time they had a night like that. She hated to think it could be their last.

His side of the bed was empty when she finally woke up. It was still early, but Wray was already gone, his clothes off the floor and the only sign he'd spent the night in the room with her the scent of him in the air. The scent of them in the air.

Stacey's thighs dampened at the smell of sex and her husband. If he was still there, she would have dragged him to the shower and had her way with him in there, but he was gone.

She tried not to tell herself that meant he was done, but as she showered and got ready for the day, she couldn't stop the sinking feeling that grew in her gut. Last night was his way of saying goodbye.

To hide the pain she knew was coming, Stacey searched her closet for something that always made her feel good. Powerful. Strong. Sexy. She started with lace panties she didn't wear often because they felt silly not to show off. She added a matching bra, again thinking she was nuts but not caring. She was going to feel good when he told her he was done. Stacey found a black wrap dress in the back of her closet. She bought it years ago and only wore it for date nights and special dinners, but it wasn't overly fancy. It fit well, and the soft fabric felt amazing against her freshly shaved skin. It didn't matter if everyone else thought she was losing it, Stacey felt good. She needed the armor to face her husband.

The boys' bedroom doors were open, and they were both missing when Stacey left her room. She heard their voices mixed with Wray's in the kitchen as she carried her heels for the day downstairs and set them by the front door.

"Mommy, you look pwetty," Evan said when Stacey walked into the kitchen.

"Why are you dressed like that?" Joey asked.

Stacey smiled at her boys and ignored her husband. She couldn't look at his face and see dismissal or even a question, so she focused on her sons. "Thank you, Evan. And Joey, I just felt like wearing a dress today. Why are you wearing that shirt?"

"Because superheroes are awesome," Joey said simply.

"They are. And you feel powerful when you wear a superhero shirt. I feel good when I wear a dress."

"But you never wear a dress," Joey said.

"Your mom looks stunning in a dress, and if it makes her feel like she can do anything, it's all the more reason for her to wear one," Wray said to Joey, brushing past Stacey to deposit pancakes on the boys' plates. When he turned to go back to the stove, his gaze scanned her body and met hers with a heated look that had her rethinking wearing something as thin and flimsy as lace panties.

"Thank you," Stacey breathed, unable to say more.

Wray went back to the stove and continued with the pancakes. Stacey poured herself a cup of coffee and debated her own breakfast for the day.

"Blueberries, because I know they're your favorite," Wray said, offering her a plate.

Stacey met his gaze and nodded. She took the plate. "Thank you."

"You look stunning," he said quietly, so the boys didn't hear.

"Thank you."

He winked at her and turned her toward the table. He went back to his pancakes, and she shuffled to the table and sat between the boys.

They all acted like nothing was different. The boys argued and groaned when Wray sent them upstairs to brush their teeth before leaving for school. Wray had lunches packed and backpacks ready to go. He even had lunch packed for Stacey, something he rarely did.

"Thank you," she said.

Wray grinned widely. "Is that the only thing you're going to say to me today? Not that I don't appreciate it, but I think I owe you a few thank you's, too." He leaned in close and whispered in her ear, "My thighs are still sore from that last time, but it was so worth it to watch you do that."

Stacey's lace panties were done for. She was going to need to change them before she left the house. But they definitely did their job and made her feel sexy. She nearly moaned at Wray's words. "You were gone when I got up. I thought you..."

Wray groaned and pressed himself against her. "I'm sorry. I heard the boys and knew you'd be up soon. I figured it would be easier on you if I handled them. I didn't think you'd worry about me regretting last night or anything. I loved every second of it."

"Are you sure?"

"Fuck, yes, Stacey. I love you. I know I have a lot of work to do to prove that to you and earn back your trust and love, but I'm here. I'm not going anywhere. And if you decide you're done and you really want me to move out, I'm still not giving up on proving to you that I'm a changed man. I love you."

Stacey's heart hitched at his words. She wanted so badly to believe him and to forgive him and for it all to be okay, but it wasn't that simple. Life wasn't that simple. She loved him and knew that would never change, but trust was a different story.

"I'll see you tonight. Are you sure you're okay with not moving out?"

"Absolutely," he said, taking a step back.

She saw the recognition in his gaze. He knew she wasn't going to forgive and forget so easily. But there was something else there. Something that was new. Determination. He wasn't giving up. And that thought sent a tingle down her spine.

THREE DAYS LATER, Wray was lying on his bunk at work and sexting with his wife. A month ago, he never thought that would happen, but he had the proof right there in blue and gray bubbles.

It started out as innocent texts about the boys and their evening since Wray had to report that morning and didn't see them after school. He hated working weekends, but it was part of the job. He knew it didn't matter when he worked, he still missed his family. Which was why he always asked Stacey about their day and what happened.

She filled him in on school and their stories from the day. She told him a little about her day and the client of hers that was moving out the following week. And then she told him she missed having him in the bed with her.

All week, she was waiting in the bedroom after Wray finished reading a story to the boys. She told him to come in so they could talk, then they spent the night not talking. Not that Wray was complaining.

He figured when he was at work, Stacey would be more willing to talk. They couldn't have sex if they weren't in the same room, and they had things to talk about. To work out. But he was wrong about one thing. Stacey could definitely have sex without him there. He was the only one who was out of luck.

Wray debated leaving his bunk and going to the bathroom, but with people wandering the halls at all hours and no telling when an alarm would go off, Wray couldn't get himself off.

But damn, did he want to.

Wray: How wet are you?
Stacey: Slippery.

Wray: Do you have a vibrator?

Stacey: No. I always felt weird about that. I mean, I had you.

Stacey: I mean have you.

Wray tried not to let the slip hurt, but it did. For months, she didn't have him, and he wasn't sure if she did now. He was more than willing, but she hadn't forgiven him and he wasn't sure she ever would.

Wray: Maybe it would be good for nights like this. You can press the vibrator to your clit. Let it get you off. Slide it deep into your pussy and fuck yourself hard like I would if I were there.

Stacey: Oh, God, Wray. I'm close. I wish I could hear your voice.

Wray: I wish I could see you. I wish I was there with you to fuck you hard and feel you come on my dick.

Stacey: Fuck, Wray.

Wray: Don't hold back, Stace. Rub your clit with your fingers. Slide that slippery come all over your pussy. Fuck yourself with your fingers, then slide them up and pinch your clit. Let yourself go. Come for me, baby. Come.

Stacey: Oh, Godddddddddddddd

Wray pulsed in his shorts, barely holding back as his cock throbbed and he waited for her to text again.

Stacey: It's better when you're here.

Wray: Always. I'll be back soon.

Stacey: I can't wait.

Wray: You should get some sleep.

Stacey: Yeah, I guess. I'm worn out now.
We'll talk tomorrow.
    Wray: I love you.
    Stacey: Me, too.

Wray was less than thrilled with that response, but it was better than no response at all.

"What are you doing?" Braden asked from the cot next to Wray's.

"What do you mean?"

"You're moving around. I'm trying to sleep over here."

"Sorry. I was just texting Stacey."

"Is everything okay?"

"Yeah. Fine. Good."

"That's new. What's going on?"

"We're... trying, I guess."

"What the hell does that mean?"

"It means we're trying to find a way back to each other."

"That's great, man." Braden waited a beat. "Why don't you sound happier about it?"

"I am. I'm just... It's different. I'm trying to be better, and I am, but I don't know if she's willing to forgive me."

"She hasn't?"

"No. She won't say she loves me either."

Braden sucked in a breath. "That's not good. Sorry."

"Yeah, thanks. But I mean, it'll get better. We'll figure it out. Sorry I was keeping you up."

"No worries. I'll—"

The alarm went off, interrupting Braden's sentence and rousing all of them. Braden followed Wray out of the bunk room and down to the truck and they went to work, everything else forgotten while they put everything into doing their jobs.

10

––––––––––

STACEY DROVE PAST THE STREET WHERE HOLLY'S BODY WAS found for the third afternoon in a row. She'd gotten into the habit of taking detours on her way to and from work to try to find Oscar. She drove by his house in the morning, drove by where Holly was killed in the afternoon, and if she took a lunch break, she drove by where Oscar supposedly worked.

She hadn't seen him. In days. It was like he'd just vanished.

She called Vera's school to confirm she was still attending classes, even though she didn't really have the authority to do so. The woman who answered the phone knew Vera's situation and was extremely chatty, telling Stacey all about how Vera was doing since moving in with her father.

Again, it was good news and bad. Good because Vera seemed to be doing well, but bad because Stacey had no grounds to have her removed from Oscar's home.

Stacey sighed heavily, telling herself and Holly she would find the proof needed to get Vera away from Oscar. Stacey just didn't know what that proof would be or where she'd find it. But she was not going to let the girl stay with the man who killed her mother.

Even if he was her father.

Stacey's last stop of the day was to the lot where Holly's car was dumped and torched. The lot was empty the day Holly died, but when Stacey got closer, she saw lines of vehicles parked there. A sign at the entrance said Event Parking.

Stacey pulled up to the gate and rolled down her window.

"Twenty bucks," the guy collecting cash told her.

"I just wanted to ask you a question."

He jutted his chin toward her.

"How long has this lot been open?"

"It's seasonal. I mostly only open it for special occasions and stuff. I don't pay to staff it full time, so usually I keep it locked."

"A few weeks ago, a car was set on fire in this lot—"

"I didn't have anything to do with that. The cops talked to me already. I was working at my day job. A dozen people saw me and I scanned in and out that day. Plus, there are cameras that saw me there."

Stacey shook her head. "I didn't think you were involved. I was just wondering if you had any idea who it could have been."

The guy shook his head. He swiped his hat off and scratched the top of his head, then pushed his hair back and smashed the hat back into place. "Nah, I don't. The lock wasn't cut, so I'm guessing they jumped the curb. I put up cameras, but not until after. I really don't have a lot of employees or anything, so no one really hangs around here."

"Have you ever seen a guy in a light blue sedan? Dark

hair and eyes. It's an older style car, boxy shape. I'm not sure what kind."

The guy thought for a second, then shook his head. "Sorry. Doesn't sound familiar. But like I said, I'm only open for special occasions, so I don't really have regulars."

Stacey nodded. Her phone buzzed in the cupholder. She glanced at it, seeing a text from Wray. She ignored the phone and turned back to the attendant. "Thanks for your help."

"Yep, no problem. Have a good night."

Stacey nodded and turned around just past his booth. She headed back out onto the street and toward home, hating that she still didn't have answers.

It had been weeks since Holly died. Instead of helping to bring her killer to justice, Stacey handed Holly's daughter over to Holly's killer. Oscar knew Stacey knew he was guilty, but he was smarter than she gave him credit for. What she needed to figure out was how he got away with it. If he had an alibi, some of the witnesses had to know something. If she could talk to them, get them to see how dangerous he was...

Stacey shook her head at the thought. If they were willing to lie for him in the first place, why would they tell the truth now?

Stacey drove home, distracted by her thoughts about Oscar and Vera and Holly. When she got in the house, Wray was there with the boys, already eating dinner.

"You didn't wait for me?" Stacey asked.

"I sent you a text and called a while ago. I thought you would be home by now." Wray lifted a brow like he expected an answer.

"I had some errands to run," Stacey said.

"Oh, yeah? Where did you go? I could have run your errands while you were at work."

"It wasn't a big deal. I didn't mind." Stacey avoided his gaze and focused on her sons. "How were your days, boys?"

"Good," Evan said. "We had pizza for lunch today. It was dewicious."

"Pizza is always delicious. How's Ms. Stephanie doing?"

"She good. She said I smart."

"You are smart," Stacey said, ruffling his hair. He smiled up at her. He looked a lot like Wray. Dark hair and eyes, with a permanent mischievous grin.

"I got all my spelling words right," Joey said.

"Great job," Stacey said. "You've been working hard to learn your spelling words. You should be proud of the work you're doing."

Joey's smile widened with the praise. He scooped a bite of broccoli into his mouth.

"Let me get you a plate," Wray said, standing and moving across the kitchen to serve Stacey.

She watched him as he made his way around the kitchen. His movements were jerky and stiff. When he came back, he shoved the plate toward her and avoided her gaze.

The rest of the night went pretty much the same. Stacey talked to the boys, and Wray ignored her. They all watched a movie together, then it was time for the boys to go to bed.

Stacey went up to the bedroom while Wray was reading to them, as had become their routine. He was sleeping in the bedroom most nights. If she met him downstairs, he didn't follow her up, but if she went to the room, he stayed.

She took off her jewelry and washed her makeup off her face while Wray finished reading. The bruising from her altercation with Oscar was fading and almost gone finally, but the yellow stain around her eye was a reminder of how dangerous the man was.

Wray cleared his throat from the bedroom.

Stacey turned off the bathroom light and walked out. She smiled, then noticed he was standing at the door and it was still open. "Is everything okay?"

He crossed his arms over his chest. His body was tense. "I don't know. Is it?"

"What do you mean?"

"Where were you tonight?"

Stacey shifted her weight and shrugged. "I said I had errands to run."

"You did, but you never said what errands. You didn't come home with any purchases."

"Why are you giving me the third degree?"

"I just want to know where you were." His calm voice put her on edge.

"I don't know why you need to know. I don't need to tell you everything about what I do and where I go."

He nodded. "You're right. You don't." He turned toward the hallway.

"Where are you going?"

"Downstairs."

"What? Why?"

"I think that's the right thing right now."

"Because I had something to do after work today?"

He shook his head. "Because you've had something after work every day this week so far. Because you're keeping things from me. Because I want this to work, but I'm not really sure right now if you do. And I think it's better if I sleep downstairs tonight."

Stacey couldn't believe it. "You've been keeping tabs on me?"

Wray sighed heavily. "No. I've just noticed a change in your pattern. You were in a car accident, then you were attacked, and then you got a threat about our family. I am scared out of my mind when you come home later than I expect. I am scared when you leave. I'm scared when I'm not home to see that you guys are all okay. I'm scared all the damn time, but you don't seem to be worried at all. So, I'm going to sleep downstairs because I have all this nervous energy inside and I can't just fuck you and roll over and pretend everything is good right now."

Stacey scoffed at his choice of words. She wanted to argue with him. To yell. To punch something. She was uptight and angry. She'd been doing everything she could to find proof Oscar killed Holly, and instead of being free to do that, Wray was questioning her every fucking move. He wanted her to feel guilty for being out.

"Screw you," Stacey hissed.

Wray nodded, then backed out of the room, closing the door behind him.

Stacey balled up her fists and squeezed until she left imprints of her nails on her palms. Then she went back to the bathroom and turned on the shower. If she couldn't get all the frustration out with an orgasm, she'd have to cry it out in the shower.

WRAY LISTENED to Stacey in the shower. Every so often a sob would echo through the house, soft enough that it was obvious she was holding back, but loud enough for him to hear in the old house with the zero soundproofing.

Wray couldn't bring himself to ask the question he really wanted the answer to because if she answered it, he wouldn't be able to pretend he didn't know. If she admitted she was having an affair, he would leave. When they got together, cheating was the one thing they agreed on. They both said if either of them ever wanted to be with someone else, they'd end the marriage before they would ever cheat.

And until his wife started coming home late and staying out late and leaving early for work, Wray never would have thought she would cheat on him. But he couldn't come up with any other explanation. And she wasn't offering one.

The shower finally turned off. He listened for her steps as she moved across the house. Drawers opened and closed. The floorboards creaked with her movements toward the bathroom, then to the bed. When she finally laid down, Wray closed his eyes.

He wanted to be in bed with her. He wanted to be buried deep inside of her. He wanted his wife to be his again. But he couldn't do it right then. Not when he hadn't been able to come up with another reason she was not around and stayed away from him when she got home.

Wray went to the kitchen and grabbed a beer. He twisted the cap off and tossed it in the recycling, then carried the beer to the couch. He turned on the TV and found a football game from years ago being replayed. He didn't care about either team. He just stared at the nearly silent TV and drank his beer and tried to convince himself his wife was not having an affair and trying to pick a fight with him to alleviate her own guilt.

He was less than successful.

When morning came, Wray felt like shit. He only had the one beer, but he couldn't sleep. The TV was still on, and he never laid down on the couch, falling asleep in a seated position. His neck hurt like hell and his back screamed from the awkwardness. Footsteps on the stairs told him it was time to get moving, so he turned off the TV and unfolded himself from the couch just in time to have the boys turn the corner and find him in the living room.

"What are you doing here?" Joey asked.

"I fell asleep on the couch."

"Are you and Mommy fighting again?" Joey asked. "Because there's this kid in my class who said his parents fight all the time, and his dad always sleeps on the couch, but then one day his dad moved out and he never saw him again."

"That's not going to happen," Wray said firmly. He put a hand on each boy's shoulder. "I will never disappear on you guys. Or your mother. I love her and the two of you."

"But if you're fighting, you won't live here," Evan said.

"No, bud. Mommy and I are trying to work everything out. I don't want to leave."

"But Mommy wants you to leave?" Joey asked, his eyes wide.

"I didn't say that. Daddy did something really bad, and Mommy got really upset. And she should because what Daddy did isn't okay."

"Did you say you're sorry?" Evan asked.

Wray nodded. "I did."

"Then Mommy should forgived you. That's what you tell me and Joe-Joe."

"It is what we tell you, but it's not always that easy. Some things are harder to forgive than others."

"Then say it more so she'll believe you," Joey stressed.

Wray nodded. "I'll do that. But first, let's get you two some breakfast. What sounds good today?"

"Cereal!"

"Waffles."

Wray led the boys to the kitchen and started their day. If he was lucky, it would not be as long as yesterday.

STACEY BARELY SPOKE to Wray before she left for work. She was still upset and hurt, and she didn't want to get into it first thing. So, she just left.

She spent the morning going through all her files from when Holly and Vera lived at the shelter. She reread every word, every detail of what Oscar did to Holly. Stacey let the rage fill her as she remembered the look in Holly's eyes the first day they arrived, the fear and uncertainty. But the one that always got Stacey was the shame.

Shame was the biggest thing for Holly to overcome. She thought it was her fault that Oscar was so violent and abusive. Holly tried for years to defuse situations with him and to make things better, but it never lasted. Teaching her that his actions had nothing to do with her was a hard lesson to learn.

Stacey knew before Holly left that she learned that lesson. Holly no longer blamed herself for what happened with Oscar. She was determined to stay away from him, and to keep Vera safe. Before she left, Holly told Stacey she wanted a necklace, a bird, to remind her she was free.

As a gift, Stacey asked Taylor if she had something like that. She explained the situation to Taylor, and Taylor took the idea and ran with it. Stacey never told Holly where she got the necklace, but she had the notes about it in Holly's file. Stacey had forgotten about it until she saw the note. She picked up her phone to call Taylor.

"Well, hello. I don't normally hear from you during the day." Taylor's smile was clear in her voice.

"Hi, Taylor. How are you?"

"I'm good." Papers shuffled on Taylor's end. A door closed in the background, then she said, "Sorry. Jessica had stuff for me to sign. What's up? How are things with Wray?"

"Not great, but that's not why I called."

"Okay, well, we'll get to that in a minute. Why did you call?"

Stacey had known Taylor for years, and even though their friendship was based on Wray's friendship with Braden, Stacey still liked and respected Taylor. She owned her own business designing exercise clothes for plus-size women. Taylor was smart and beautiful and talented. And she was dating Dex, a former SEAL who was a badass with a mushy middle just for Taylor.

"Do you remember the necklace you gave me? For my client?"

"Yeah. Holly, right? How is she?"

"She's dead."

"What?" Taylor breathed.

Taylor and Holly never met, but when Holly told Stacey she loved birds, Stacey told her about Taylor. Taylor's company was Birds of a Feather, and her logo was a bird. She had a bird necklace custom-made for Holly. A one-of-a-kind necklace.

"I meant to tell you. The funeral was the day of the last party we came to at your house. I was still sort of in shock. Even now, I can't believe she's gone."

"I bet. Wow. I'm so sorry. I was really hoping to meet her one day."

"She was, too."

"What happened? Can I ask that?" Taylor's voice was quieter, like she was unsure about asking.

"It's still an open investigation, but I think her ex found her. He was following her."

"Has he been arrested?" Taylor blurted.

"He has an alibi."

"That's ridiculous. Do you want me to call Dex? Get F-BOMB on it?"

"No. The cops are looking into it. I'm sure they'll figure out something, eventually. She was supposed to be okay, you know? I just wanted to tell you, since you two had a connection in a way."

"Wow. Thanks for letting me know. This is just... I definitely feel like I can't ask about Wray after that news."

"It's fine. Nothing is really going on."

"That tone doesn't sound like nothing."

Stacey thought about the fight they had that morning. She knew Taylor would listen, but Stacey really didn't want to share her failings as a wife with a woman who seemed to have it all together.

"We've been trying to be okay."

"What does that mean?"

"He's been really nice lately. Helping more with the boys and doing stuff around the house. I, uh, got into an accident a couple weeks ago, and he was really nice after that. He's just been...nice."

"So you said. Anything other than nice? Because naughty can be a lot of fun, too."

Stacey's cheeks heated at the memory of the last time Wray spent the night in the bedroom with her. Her thighs tingled, and she was grateful for being on the phone instead of in person.

"There's a little of that, too."

"What? That's awesome. Good for you. I'm so happy you guys are working things out."

"Well, not entirely, but right now, we're trying to coexist."

"Good. You know I want you two back together. And I know you don't like the idea of divorce. Hopefully, you guys are back to normal soon."

Stacey smiled big enough to force the word out, "Yep." She wasn't sure what she wanted. And after their fight last night, she wasn't sure what Wray wanted either.

11

───────

WRAY SPENT THE NEXT FOUR NIGHTS ON THE COUCH. STACEY was more and more distant with each night. Wray told himself he was doing the right thing, but he hated putting separation between them. Asking her directly about an affair would end things, but pretending it wasn't happening when she was coming home late and not explaining her actions wasn't better.

Wray was in a shitty mood when he went to work, something Braden and the rest of the crew picked up on immediately.

"You know you can't bring your shit here," Lieutenant Perez said.

"I know, sir," Wray answered.

"Then why are you? It's clear something is going on. We're all putting our lives in your hands when we get on that truck. You need to be able to handle it," Perez pressed.

"Yes, sir. I can."

Perez glared at Wray for a long moment, then jerked his head at Braden. "Get it straight. Whatever the hell is going on, help him fix it."

Braden nodded and led the way toward the weight room. Wray followed behind like the puppy he was, doing exactly as he was told. Braden knew Wray would need to punch something or run or something if he was going to get out everything in his head. It was good to know each other so well. Until Braden had to force Wray to talk.

"What the hell is going on?" Braden asked ten minutes into their workout. They were punishing their bodies, but it was well worth it.

"Nothing," Wray replied, lining up in front of the speed bag. He imagined it was whoever Stacey was sleeping with.

"Bullshit."

Wray slammed his fist against the bag and turned on his best friend. "You wanna know what's going on? My wife is having an affair."

"What? No way."

Wray sighed and dropped to a bench. "How else do you explain her coming home late, not telling me where she's been, and hiding things from me?"

"Maybe she's involved in an illegal gambling ring," Braden said mirthlessly.

"Fuck you," Wray said, hating that Braden was right.

"You disappeared for entire weekends on Stacey and the kids. Did she ever ask you if you had an affair?"

Wray grumbled under his breath.

"I know it's not like Stacey, but I have a hard time believing she's screwing around on you."

"She's just distant lately. I thought things were getting better."

"After she asked you to move out?"

Wray nodded. "Yeah. She...got a threat. Something to do with work. It scared the hell out of her, but she asked me not to leave until she figured out what was going on. And when she was hurt, she let me take care of her. It was like things were better. She let me help her, and it was...it was really good."

"How good?"

Wray glared at his best friend. "Really good."

Braden's brows shot sky high. "Well, then. That's good news. When was this? A week ago?"

"Two now. Why?"

"And things have been really good since?"

Wray nodded. His cheeks warmed. He didn't talk to his friends or coworkers about his sex life because it always felt like a violation. She was his wife, not some random woman. She had his children and helped him become the man he was. She deserved his respect, and that meant not sharing intimate details of their personal life with others, even his best friend.

"But you're convinced she's sleeping with someone else."

It wasn't a question, but Wray still felt like he had to answer. "I can't come up with any other explanation."

"What did she say when you asked her?"

"I didn't ask her directly. Not that. I asked her where she'd been and what she was doing. She wouldn't tell me. Said she didn't answer to me."

"I still think there's something else going on. Did she ever find out what the threat was about? Could she be looking into it?"

"Stacey would not put the boys at risk like that."

"A year ago, I would have said the same about you." Braden leveled Wray with a glare that said all might be forgiven, but it was definitely not forgotten.

"I know I messed up. But that's even more of a reason I

don't think Stacey would. Do you really see her sneaking around in shady places and risking our family? Our boys? After what I did and how upset she's been with me?"

Braden shrugged. "I don't know. We do crazy things when we think we have a reason. I don't think it's a good idea, but I also don't know what's going on. Maybe she thinks she can find whoever is threatening your family and put a stop to it. Want me to call Dex? See if there's anything they can do to help?"

Wray shook his head. "I don't think it's anything that bad. And I can't ask them to jump in every time something happens in my house."

"If you change your mind, let me know. I'm sure he won't mind."

Wray nodded. He needed Dex and the other former SEALs to save him when he got in over his head. Wray's actions nearly got others killed. When they all got together, the SEALs were friendly and casual, but Wray never felt comfortable around them. They met him at his lowest and had to dig him out of a hole he created. He couldn't ask them to do him more favors.

"What's going on with you and Jessica?" Wray asked, changing the subject from his own love life to Braden's.

"What do you mean?" Braden asked, avoiding Wray's gaze.

"Don't give me that. You two were looking friendlier than usual at Taylor's party a few weeks ago."

Braden shrugged. "We're just talking. It's no big deal."

"Stacey likes Jessica a lot. Always says how great she is."

Braden dropped his weights and glared at Wray.

Wray held his hands up. "Just saying Jessica wouldn't be a bad one to date."

"She works for my sister."

"So?"

"If things don't go well, Taylor will kill me."

"What if things do go well?"

Braden shook his head. "My married best friend who thinks his wife is cheating on him is telling me to think positive. Good one. Plus, every relationship I've been in has ended. Every single one."

Wray snorted. "That's how it is for everyone until you find the one you're supposed to be with."

"Yeah, and how's that going right now? You think Stacey's not it for you?"

Wray scowled and yanked a pair of dumbbells off the rack.

"I like Jessica. She's beautiful and smart and funny. I didn't want to tell you this, but we're supposed to go out Friday night. I might cancel, though. It feels like a risk."

"Uh oh, there he is."

Braden looked over his shoulder, then turned back to Wray with a confused look.

"I meant you. You don't like risk. Ever. You want things to stay exactly in line. Jessica is a risk because she works for your sister. That woman Stacey introduced you to a while ago was a risk because she knew Stacey. Everyone is a risk. And your dating pool is going to consist of people who know the other people you know. At some point, you need to decide if someone is worth the risk."

"Yeah, yeah," Braden said.

Wray wanted to keep pushing him, but the alarm went off and they had to catch a ride.

"You good?" Lieutenant Perez asked Wray as he pulled on his turnout gear.

Wray nodded.

Perez looked over at Braden and raised a brow.

"He's better. He can watch my back."

Wray sucked in a breath at the rush of emotion. Braden was trusting him to keep him safe in whatever situation they were going into. There was no higher compliment than that.

When they got to the scene, the building was already engulfed in flames. Wray filed out of the truck with the others, waiting for their orders and staring up at the fire as it raced up the building and popped out windows like they were made of bubblegum.

Glass shattered on the ground next to the building. Crews raced to clear the area before anyone was injured.

"What the hell happened?" Perez asked Monroe, the fire captain in charge.

"We think this was a stash house for trafficking. PD got a tip on it, but when they got here, it was up in flames and we were already on the way."

"Anyone inside?" Perez asked.

Monroe shook his head. "Not that we've found. Right now, it's a matter of keeping the fire contained to this building only."

"Are the others evacuated?"

Monroe nodded. "Vacant mostly. One is an office building, where our call came from. We already got everyone out of there."

"Good. Where do you need us?"

"South side. Get some more lines over there and make sure we don't let anything jump."

"Will do, sir," Perez said. He turned to the crew and started dispersing them to help with the fire. Wray and Braden paired up on the end of a hose on one corner of the building.

"This is a big damn building to be holding people in," Braden said.

Wray looked up at the windows above them. At least a dozen, probably closer to twenty. Twenty floors of space for someone to hold people against their will. "How the hell did the people in the office building not know what was going on?"

"People don't always want to see what's right in front of them," Braden said. "Something like this is too horrible to imagine, and to think you're witnessing it is unfathomable."

"True." Wray repositioned the hose and hit a hot spot. "I hope no one's left inside."

Braden shook his head. "They wouldn't leave evidence behind."

"I wonder how they found out the cops were coming."

"Someone had to tell them," Braden said.

"That's what we're afraid of," Captain Patrick said from right behind Wray.

Wray nodded to Marcus. Their relationship was friendly over the years, but after what Wray put Stacey through, and Frannie as a consequence, Marcus didn't seem as friendly as he once was.

"Any idea who it could be?" Wray asked.

"That's why I wanted to talk to you two." Marcus was not one to pull any punches.

"I didn't know anything about this until we pulled up. And I wasn't driving," Wray defended himself.

"Good." Marcus looked at Braden for confirmation.

"He's telling the truth. We were together from when our shift started until the call came in."

"I hate that I have to ask," Marcus said, "but I wouldn't be doing my job if I didn't."

"We heard no one was inside. Is that true?" Braden asked.

"As far as we can tell. It's a big building to search, and it was already burning when we got here. By the time the first truck arrived, it was impossible to search the whole place."

Wray looked up at the building. His stomach turned at the thought of someone being taken from their lives, likely raped and abused, then killed in a fire. No one deserved that.

"Fuck," Braden breathed.

"Yeah, pretty much." Marcus stared up at the building for a long minute. "Listen, if you two hear anything, let me know."

Wray and Braden nodded.

"Any update on the threat Stacey got?" Wray asked before Marcus walked away.

"No, but I don't expect we'll find anything. The call came in from a burner. Hasn't been found or turned on again. The threat was pretty vague, unfortunately. And with what they do, it's going to happen. These men have no compassion for others. They don't care who they have to go through to get what they want."

"Gee, that makes me feel better," Wray said wryly.

Marcus shrugged. "I get it. I don't like when Frannie gets threats, but it comes with the territory."

"I don't like it."

"No, but it means they're helping someone if they're keeping a woman away from a man like that."

Wray couldn't deny that. He didn't want his wife or sons

to get hurt, but he didn't want to hand a woman over to a man who would threaten someone's family, either.

Someone called Marcus away, and he left Wray and Braden to fight the fire. They held their line on their section of the building and watched behind them for any danger at the other building.

It felt like hours before they got a break. Water and a rest before right back into it. When the fire was finally out, their crew took the lead on going inside. Water dripped from everywhere. Hot spots glowed as they moved around, targeting them with hoses and extinguishers to ensure more damage didn't occur.

Wray and Braden worked their way up the southeast stairs. The steel framework was still intact, and the treads were in decent shape. Better than some of the floors they passed that were completely burned out.

They made it to the top floor, searching the area they were given to search. They were almost done when Braden stopped. He drew back, then grabbed his radio.

"Found a body."

OSCAR CLOSED the steel door and flipped the latch closed. The whimpers from inside were almost as bad as the smell. Fucking hell. He preferred guns to people. But when he got the call that Damon needed help, he was not going to say no.

The van Oscar loaded up with women at the warehouse was not big enough for all of them. All he was told was to get over there immediately and get them all in the van. They had to sit two or three to a seat with more on the floor and some in the back. He got everyone in, but it was not a pretty picture.

The stench of them nearly made Oscar sick, but he knew being trusted with something new was a good thing. It meant Damon was seeing Oscar's value in the Company. He was important.

Oscar slammed his hand against the door and grinned when the women inside shrieked. He chuckled. Maybe there was something he enjoyed more about women. Guns didn't get scared. Women did.

Holly was scared. He got hard just thinking about the look in her eyes when he dragged her out of her car. Nothing would ever be as satisfying as killing her.

Leaving the van in the same building where the women were was not a good idea. Damon said to get rid of it when he was done. With all those women, DNA would be everywhere in it, so lighting it up was the only option.

Oscar drove down the side roads to the lot where he left Holly's car. It wasn't dark out, so there was a big risk leaving the vehicle there, but he'd done it before and had no issues at all.

The scorch mark from Holly's car was mostly gone. The gravel that covered the lot had been disturbed by other traffic. It was a lot that was never used, but it was easy enough to jump the curb and cut through the lot. The van would be found, but there wouldn't be any way to tie it back to Oscar.

He got out of the van and pulled his hat low. Even without cameras in the area, Oscar wasn't going to take any chances. He was wearing a black hoodie with no logos on it, jeans that were sold at every big box store in the country, and sneakers that left no discernible marks on the ground. He was as close to invisible as possible.

Oscar tipped over the gasoline container in the backseat

of the van. He made sure the fabric in the front and third row had enough to light instantly, then he left the container in the backseat so it would burn up with the rest of the van.

He lit a rolled up paper and tossed it into the van. Fire immediately whooshed to life. Oscar closed the door, double checking the windows were open just a crack. Enough oxygen to keep the fire going but not so much that it would go out before the entire vehicle was engulfed.

Oscar hated that he couldn't hang around and watch his handiwork, but he needed to get out of there before someone saw it and called it in. He got back to the entrance to the parking lot before he noticed the new booth. The same rusted chain hung across the entrance, but the booth to the side wasn't there last time.

Oscar looked around. His heart thumped hard in his chest. The fire was clearly visible through the windows of the van. He needed to go. But what else did he miss? Was there anything—

"Fuck," he mumbled out loud.

The telephone pole at the road had a brand new camera on it. A camera that pointed right at the entrance. A camera that Oscar was definitely on as he drove into the lot.

He looked around for something he could use to climb up to where the camera was mounted. Not much was there. He thought about throwing something, but that would only break the camera, not destroy whatever footage it captured.

He dug out his phone, but there was no one he could call. Damon would be very unhappy if Oscar messed this up. And there wasn't anyone else.

Sirens screamed in the distance, getting closer with every staccato beat of Oscar's heart. He had to take a chance that the camera wasn't good enough to see his face. It was on the passenger side, so it was very possible it didn't get him in the shot. And he'd kept his hood up and his face down the entire time since he got out of the van.

There was no way they'd know it was him. Unless they caught him in the lot watching the van burn.

He had to go. It would all be fine. He'd figure it out. And worst case, Damon would help. Oscar just hoped he didn't have to ask.

12

———————

Wray and Braden were rolling up hoses when Marcus pulled into the parking lot. He saw them and came over.

"Twice in one day. I don't like these kind of odds," Marcus said.

"Neither do we, Captain," Braden said.

"What's worse is this van looks like it matches the witness description of the one that left the scene of the earlier fire." Marcus stared at the smoking heap of metal.

Wray didn't envy the man his job. Having to not only figure out what happened to the rest of the women who were in that building, and the dead one Braden and Wray found, but what happened to the van and who set the fires. Wray just put them out, then he got to leave and forget about it until the next one.

Most of the time. He wouldn't forget finding that body anytime soon.

"Do you think this van carried away more people who were being held in that building?" Braden asked.

"It's the working theory. They lit it up because it destroys all the DNA inside that could have told us who any of the women were."

"What did the witness see?" Braden asked.

"She heard a horn being blasted over and over. That was what drew her attention to the building. She looked out but couldn't see anything, but before she left the window, a van pulled out of the building. Took off like it was already on fire."

"Was it?" Wray asked.

Marcus shook his head. "She's the one who reported the fire, though. She saw it a little while later. That's why she mentioned the van."

"Any idea who the woman was?" Braden asked.

Braden took finding the body harder than Wray, but it wasn't a good sight. The woman was near one of the windows like she'd been trying to get fresh air. Braden asked Wray if he thought the woman called out and no one heard her over the sound of the fire. It was possible, but it was horrible to imagine. The woman's skin had melted off her, and she was huddled on her side with some kind of fabric stuck to her body. She tried to survive, but she couldn't. If she'd been held as a trafficking victim, she probably hoped she could escape the building after the others left, but the fire was too hot by then and she was trapped.

"Nothing yet," Marcus said. "Those things take time. But we're going to run everything through missing persons. We're not going to get anything from this van, unfortunately."

"Hey, Captain?" Lieutenant Perez said as he approached.

"Hate to see all of you again."

"Me, too, but I wanted to point out that there's a camera on this lot."

"What?" Marcus barked. He turned around until he

noticed where Perez was pointing. "Do we know who owns this lot?"

Perez shook his head. "I wouldn't know, sir. The camera looks fairly new. There's also a building over there that looks like it's new. Someone might be trying to use this as more than a dumping ground."

"Dumping ground?" Marcus asked.

Perez shrugged. "We put out a fire a few weeks ago in the same spot. Another vehicle. Ended up belonging to that woman who was killed. Carjacking. Guess the person who did it knew this place was empty."

Marcus nodded, looking around the lot.

Wray tried to see what Marcus was seeing. All he saw was an empty space with nothing to deter people from using it however they saw fit. Whoever owned it needed to be smarter about blocking off access to the lot if they were going to avoid suspicion. One chain clearly wasn't enough to stop people from driving right in.

"Thanks. I'll look into this. And get that footage. You mind if I stop by and talk to these two later? Since they found the body?" Marcus asked.

Perez shook his head. "Not at all, sir."

Marcus nodded. "Thanks. I'll see you all later." He was already on his phone and barking orders to find the owner before he even made it back to his car.

"I guess this is as good a place as any to light up a car. Pretty vacant area. Not a business in sight. I wonder what they use the lot for," Braden said.

"No clue. I don't remember being here before," Wray said.

"Me either."

Perez called them over to finish loading up their gear, then they headed back to the station. They cleaned up and were getting food when Marcus arrived with questions.

"Either of you recognize this man?" Marcus asked. He turned the tablet to face them so they could see the screen.

A man walked toward the exit of the lot. He was in a dark sweatshirt and jeans, his face hidden from view. He stopped and looked at the small building near the entrance, then turned and looked around the lot. He moved closer to the camera, out of view of it, his face hidden the entire time.

"That's it?" Braden asked.

Marcus nodded.

"He never looks up at the camera?" Wray asked.

"We're guessing he noticed the building, then spotted the camera and made sure he was out of the view before he studied it. He doesn't come back into view."

"That could be anyone," Braden said.

"It could be you," Wray told him.

Braden nodded. "I'm pretty sure I have a black sweatshirt and jeans somewhere. Whoever he is, he was smart about what he was wearing."

"Yeah, he was. But eventually, they always end up getting stupid," Marcus said.

"Why did you think we might know him?" Wray asked.

Marcus shook his head. "I'm asking everyone in the department. I looked into the fire Perez mentioned was there a few weeks ago, and I wanted to talk to you first."

"Me? Why?" Wray asked. His palms tingled with sweat. The back of his neck stiffened with fear. His mouth went dry.

"The car from a few weeks ago? It was Stacey's client's car."

"Oh, shit," Wray breathed.

"What does that mean?" Braden asked.

"We don't know," Marcus answered. "Stacey's client was killed in an apparent carjacking. We went hard after the husband, but he had an alibi. A good one that included witnesses. We had to let him go, even though I'm not convinced he wasn't involved. He's the one who attacked Stacey."

"Wait, what?" Wray blurted. "You know who attacked her and you didn't do anything? He put a knife to my wife's fucking throat!"

"I know, but there were no witnesses. Stacey didn't want to press charges. She didn't see him, just spoke to him, so she can't even be a witness herself. If I went after him, especially after we went after him for his wife's death, he could turn around and sue the police department."

"Fuck the police department. That's my damn wife. You're going to let this asshole walk around when he put a knife to her throat and nearly broke her arm. He terrified her. Is he the one who threatened her on the phone?"

Marcus sighed. "We think it's likely."

"So there have been two instances where this man went after my wife, and you haven't done anything?"

"Three actually," Marcus said.

"Three?"

"Stacey was following him when she got into her accident. Said he swerved, and that's why she swerved and hit that car."

"Fucking hell, Marcus! What are you doing? Stacey is in danger. She's getting threats, our sons are in danger, and you know who's doing this and won't do a damn thing."

"I can't. I have zero proof. The witness at the accident said there were people in the crosswalk that the driver swerved to avoid. The guy at the drive-thru never saw anyone else. And the threat was called in from a burner phone that's likely at the bottom on the gorge by now. I have nothing."

Wray ran a hand over his head and down the back of his neck. He wanted to punch something. Or scream. Do something that would fix this. His wife. His fucking wife. And Marcus wasn't doing anything.

"Is that what this guy looks like?" Braden asked, drawing Marcus and Wray's attention.

Wray looked up at Marcus.

"I can't see this man well enough to say for sure. Do you know what he looks like?" Marcus asked.

Wray shook his head. "No. I don't know who you're talking about at all."

Marcus nodded. "He fits the height and general size, but that's not enough for me to use for a warrant."

"So, he's going to get away with even more?" Wray snapped.

"I'm doing the best I can," Marcus growled. "I don't want to let this go anymore than you want me to, but I have to work inside the law."

"Fucking ridiculous," Wray mumbled.

"I just came to see if you two could help. I'll be going to see Frannie and Stacey next." Marcus snapped the tablet case closed and glared at Wray before walking out.

Braden turned to Wray. "Do you think that could be where Stacey's been? Following that guy?"

All the anger Wray felt toward Marcus deflated. Stacey was a protector. She was a mama bear for their boys, and even for him at times. She loved her patients so much that she'd be in tears for them. When Holly died, Stacey blamed herself.

Could Wray imagine her following the husband? Especially if she thought the husband was to blame for Holly's death?

Absolutely.

And it needed to stop.

STACEY TRIED to stop her entire body from shaking, but she couldn't. She stared at Marcus as he left the office, hating that she couldn't bring herself to lie and say it was Oscar in the video. It could have been. It probably was. But to swear under oath in a court of law that it was? Stacey couldn't.

She'd witnessed too much pain at the hands of people who thought they didn't have to follow the rules to be a part of that. She wanted to take Oscar down, to have him pay for what he did, but she wasn't going to do anything illegal in order to make it happen.

Not without proof.

Which she still didn't have.

Frannie walked back into the office and closed the door. She sat behind her desk and folded her hands in front of her. "I'm sorry he put you in that position."

"I wish I'd been able to say it was him."

"You aren't the type to cheat the system."

"No, but I'm not above encouraging the system in the right direction," Stacey said.

"I get that. More than you know. Sometimes the system isn't fair. Sometimes it protects the wrong people. But if we're willing to do the things they're willing to do, we're no better than they are."

"I'm not willing to kill others," Stacey said firmly.

"I know. But you're also not willing to take a father away from a child who just lost her mother unless you can prove he did what we know he did. Because if you do, you and I both know he'll be right back where he is now and with an even bigger chip on his shoulder and more confidence in his ability to evade the cops. Vera is more important than that. She needs a safe home for good, not for now."

Stacey nodded. She put her head in her hands. "I know. I just hate the thought of what he might be doing to her."

"He's not that stupid."

Stacey snorted.

Frannie laughed with her. "I didn't say he's not stupid. I said he's not that stupid. He knows she's being watched by half the county right now. He's not going to do anything that puts him in view of anyone else, and if that child has a head cold without cause, he's going to be questioned. I guarantee it."

Stacey drew a big breath and let it out slowly, finally calming her pulse. "Do you think it was him? Do you think he's dumb enough to go back to where he ditched Holly's car and dump another one?"

Frannie considered for a second, then nodded. "I think he's cocky. He got away with Holly's murder, so far, and he thinks he's untouchable. Whatever he's doing, he thinks no one is going to take him down."

"What do you think he's doing?"

Frannie shook her head. "I don't know for sure, but my guess is he's a runner for a trafficking ring."

"What?"

Frannie leaned forward. "Do you remember Angelica? She was here when you were on maternity leave with Evan, so you only saw her once or twice."

Stacey nodded. "I vaguely remember her, yes. Why?"

"She was a victim of human trafficking. She got away and

came here, but she was afraid of her own shadow. Rightfully so. It was hard for her to imagine a life that was normal. And after the things she talked about, I couldn't blame her. This sounds similar to some of the things she talked about. A large abandoned space, no contact with anyone, but someone always seemed to be watching. Fires to hide DNA evidence. She had scars from when she tried to stay behind once. She waited until she thought she was safe, but someone was there, like they knew she didn't go with the others. It was horrible."

"And you think this is what Oscar is involved in?"

Frannie shrugged. "It definitely seems that way if that was him in the video."

"We need to find proof. If he goes away for this, it's something. It's not justice for Holly, but it'll get Vera away from him for good."

"I agree." Frannie leveled Stacey with a stare and drew a breath. "I have something for you. It's something I've never given anyone else, or shown to anyone else. It's something I'm proud of and scared of."

"What is it?" Stacey asked.

Frannie opened her second desk drawer. She moved something to the side, then lifted out a simple wooden box. She set it on her desk and smoothed her hands over the surface. She opened it, flipping the lid all the way back and revealing a black mask. The kind people wore to masquerade balls, but simple, with no beading or feathers or adornment.

"A mask?"

"Before I started Shelter in the Storm, I worked as an exotic dancer. The club is long gone, but we wore these masks. On my way home one night, I witnessed a young woman's murder. I didn't do anything. I ran. My friend and I ran. But I couldn't shake the guilt I felt and talked to the cops. To Marcus."

"What happened?"

"It's a long story, but helping Marcus with that case led me to open this place. It led me to Marcus. It showed me just how strong I can be if I need to be. I can still see the killer's face. He haunts me. Dark hair and eyes with a scar across his right eyebrow. The man was evil personified. I've never been so scared in my life as the day I came face to face with him."

"Oh, my God," Stacey breathed.

"This mask gave me the strength to face him. I know that sounds trite, but it's true. This mask made me feel like a true vigilante, taking down bad guys and solving crimes. I don't think I would have had the courage to face him without the strength I got from this silly piece of fabric."

"Really?"

Frannie nodded and lifted the mask from the box. She looked at it as though she saw something else. Maybe someone else. Then she handed it over to Stacey.

"What do you want me to do?"

"This is yours now. You are already doing the work. You're going after Oscar. You're going to figure out what he's involved in and take him down. I hope this gives you the strength to keep going when you're not sure. The red tape of bureaucracy isn't always protecting the right people, and sometimes we need to take matters into our own hands."

"Frannie, I'm not sure that's a good idea."

"Why not?"

"My boys. Wray. I can't put them at risk."

"These people, people like Oscar, they're not going to sit back and let you walk away. When they think you know something, they'll come after you. Every time."

"Did they come after you?"

Frannie nodded. "Yep."

"What did you do?"

"I fought back. I made sure I was smarter than they were."

Stacey took the mask and turned it over in her hand. It wasn't fancy or special. It had remnants of glitter on it, but it was a plain black mask. The kind you can get from anywhere.

"You don't have to take it. You don't have to do anything. You can let Marcus and the rest of the police department figure out what happened. But you and I both know Marcus can't touch Oscar right now. Not without something new. Which means he gets to walk around right now and Holly is in a grave."

Stacey drew a breath and leaned back. "It's not right."

"No, it's not."

"I don't know if I can do anything."

"I've sat back and watched you with this. I never wanted to tell you about this. As long as we've known each other, I never thought I would. But seeing the look in your eyes today, I recognize that look. It's the same one I had. You're not going to rest until you find the proof Holly insists is there. I don't want you to get hurt, but I know I'm not going to be able to stop you."

"You sound like you're trying to talk me into this."

Frannie chuckled. "I had a friend who tried to talk me out of it. She was with me when the woman was killed. Gwen was the one who said we should run. We were scared, and drunk, and Gwen knew the police wouldn't trust our word. But after a few days, Gwen wanted to help. She tried. We both did. Sitting with that memory wasn't something we could handle, just like sitting with the belief that Oscar killed Holly isn't something you can handle. I see it. I know that's how it is. And I don't want to talk you into anything, but I want you to be safe if you do it, anyway."

"And a mask will make me safe?"

"No. A mask will make you a badass. A curvy vigilante badass."

Stacey smiled at her boss and nodded. "I like the sound of that."

"Are you going to take the mask?"

Stacey lifted it to her face and looked through it. Her vision was focused. Ready. She was definitely a badass.

"Yeah, I'll take it."

13

———

Oscar fucked up. He knew he did, and getting a summons in the middle of the night confirmed it. He left Vera a note that something came up and he had to go out, then left his house and hoped he'd get the chance to return.

The warehouse was busy in the middle of the night. Oscar had never seen so many people there. There were trucks outside and people walking around with clipboard and barking orders at people driving forklifts. Oscar thought the whole thing was just for show, but witnessing the activity proved there was a lot more going on than he knew about within the Company.

He stepped in front of the two men guarding Damon's door and met their gazes. Neither of them ever looked particularly friendly, but their matching steely gazes sent a chill up Oscar's spine that settled in his throat and squeezed tight.

One of the men knocked twice on the door, then opened it and stepped to the side. He nodded to Oscar and raised a brow when Oscar didn't immediately go inside. If he thought he had any other option, he would have gotten the hell out of there.

"Get your ass in here. Now," Damon bellowed. Even above the noise of the warehouse, his anger came through loud and clear.

Oscar couldn't fix the fact that he was caught on camera, but since no one had shown up at his door, he figured either the cops couldn't identify him or the camera was a fake. None of that would matter to Damon, though. Damon didn't tolerate excuses.

"What was your task today?" Damon asked, his condescending tone accompanied by a tilt of his head like Oscar was a rotten child.

"To pick up the women and get them all to the new place."

"And how many women did I tell you to pick up?"

"All of them?"

"Are you asking me or telling me?" Damon glared harder.

"All of them, sir."

"And how many was that?"

Oscar tried to remember. Damon said get them all. Did he say how many? "Uh, I'm not sure."

"Well, let me make the math really fucking simple for you. It's one more than you got."

"What?" Oscar's eyes went wide.

"You left one woman behind."

"I did what you asked. I went there, I pulled inside. And I got all of them. I couldn't have left one. Why would one stay?"

"She stayed upstairs. Must have figured she could escape once you were gone with the others."

Oscar's heart sank. If one got out, she could talk. She could tell the cops everything. She could identify him.

"I didn't know. I didn't know someone was left behind. What did she say? Did she tell the cops anything?"

"She's dead. Died in the fire. But they have her body. And dead people have stories. Dead people have histories. Dead people are found, and their pasts are pieced together."

Oscar swallowed roughly. If she died, she couldn't identify him. That was the only time he'd been involved in trafficking women, and he didn't do anything besides drive the van. But Damon...

"As soon as they figure out who she is, they will know where she came from. They will know everything about her life before she was brought into the Company. We can't allow that to happen."

"What does that mean?"

"It means you fucked up and created more work for us."

"I can fix it. Let me—"

"It's already being handled by someone more competent than you. Someone who doesn't fuck things up all the time."

"I didn't—"

"Are you still being followed?"

"No. That bitch backed off after I saw her at the drive-thru."

"So getting rid of the van was not an issue?" Damon asked.

Oscar nodded. "Yeah. Of course. Easy."

Damon's eyes narrowed. His gaze zeroed in on Oscar's hands. He clutched them together, trying to still the need to fidget. "What happened?"

"Nothing. All good."

"Where did you leave the van?"

"An empty parking lot."

"Which one?"

"Um, up on Forty-Ninth Avenue."

"Is that the same one where you left your wife's car?" Damon growled.

"Uh, yeah. I figured it was a good spot last time, so—"

"It's been purchased since then. And has a camera installed."

Oscar shifted his weight, anxious and ready to bolt if he had to. Not that he expected a warning if Damon intended to kill him, or to actually get away, but he wasn't going to stand there and make it easy for the bastard. "I saw that when I was leaving."

"You mean after you drove onto the lot and lit the van on fire? So there's video footage of you?"

"There's no way anyone will know it's me. I was completely covered."

Damon stood and threw a glass across the room. It shattered on the wall as he shouted, "And you don't think they'll look at you first? After all, it's the same place your wife's car was left. Isn't that coincidental?"

"They cleared me for that," Oscar mumbled.

"No. They couldn't find proof you did it. There's a difference. That doesn't mean they aren't watching you or checking up on you. Having you here is a liability for the Company, but I thought I'd try to give you a chance. Let you prove what you're capable of. And instead, all I've gotten is half-ass work and excuses."

"I'll do better. I promise. I can do this."

"Can you? Because you already had one person following you. You could have the police after you. And now you were too fucking stupid to find a new place to get rid of the vehicle you used to transport sixteen women. Not seventeen like it should have been. Because you left one behind instead of doing your fucking job!"

Oscar shrunk against the wall. He wanted to run, just get the hell out of there and never come back, but that wouldn't fix anything. He knew too much. He was in, even if he wasn't all the way in. If he tried to get out, they'd kill him.

Damon drew a deep breath and let it out slowly. He tugged down his suit coat and smoothed his hands over the front. He adjusted his collar and cracked his neck with a twist. Then he met Oscar's gaze.

"The woman is still looking into you. She has a connection in the police department. It won't take long for them to put everything together and figure out you're the one who drove the van and the one who killed your wife. You need to make sure this woman does not keep looking. I know women like her. They think they owe it to society to find men like us. But they don't. If she wants to live, she needs to back off. If I find out she follows you again, you won't get another chance. Put an end to this. Now."

Oscar nodded and backed out of the room. He ducked his head as he walked past the guards and hurried through the warehouse, only stopping when someone dropped something and he almost pissed himself.

Oscar slammed the door of his car and gripped the steering wheel tight. He sucked in deep breaths, trying to slow his racing heart. When he finally did, he knew exactly what he needed to do to prove himself to Damon.

And to secure his place in the Company.

Stacey was always happy to see women move out of Shelter in the Storm. It was a celebration, an accomplishment. It meant they were confident in their new skills and not willing to return to the men who sent them there in the first place.

But after Holly, Stacey hated to see them go. Raina was a lot like Holly. Both were strong women, but they got sucked into a world they didn't know existed and by the time they figured out what was going on, they were so deep they couldn't get out. It took both of them a long time to find their internal strength to even try to leave. And when they did, they looked over their shoulders at every turn.

Both came through it as new women. They were stronger than ever before. But Holly still wasn't free. She wanted to be, and she tried to be, but Oscar found her. There was no way in hell Stacey was going to let the same thing happen to Raina, or anyone else.

She made sure Wray was going to pick up the boys since his shift ended before school was out, then Stacey made plans to stop in and see Raina before going home. Just to check on things.

The apartment building Raina and Karli lived in was relatively new. There was a secured exterior door and cameras in the entrance. Two elevators sat at the back of the entryway with open staircases on either side for residents and guests who wanted to walk.

Stacey took the elevator up and planned to walk down the stairs so she could check both out. The elevator opened onto a brightly lit hallway lined with dark carpet that muffled her footsteps as she walked toward Karli's door. Stacey turned the corner and found Karli's door three from the end.

Stacey knocked, smiling when she heard music inside the apartment. A minute later, the door swung open to a smiling Raina.

"Stacey! Come in!"

Stacey stepped inside and smiled when Raina locked the door behind her. "How are you?"

"Good," Raina said with a big breath. "It's weird being out of the shelter, but it was time for me to move on."

"How are things going here with Karli?"

"She's awesome. I hate that I missed so many years of friendship, but I'm happy we've been able to reconnect again."

"Good. Are you two fixing dinner? Something smells amazing." Stacey put her hand over her rumbling stomach.

"We are. Karli wasn't sure if it would be okay for her to be here when we talked, so she's making herself scarce in the kitchen."

"It's completely fine. I just wanted to check on you. Make sure you're still doing well." Stacey smiled at Raina and hoped it was believable. Stacey had never before worried about a client after they left. They got out, escaped from whatever hell they'd been in, and they were free. But Stacey had a bad feeling Raina was no more free than Holly had been.

"I'm good. I want to start looking for a new job. I used to be a massage therapist. Technically, I still am, but I haven't done it in years. I don't really have a lot of contacts left in the field, and I'm not sure the kind of job I want to get."

"We have career counseling services we can connect you with. You never mentioned that before, so I never brought it up, but that's something we can do for you."

"That would be great. Damon isolated me from everything else, so it's been a while since I've been able to think for myself. I like that I'm not alone anymore."

Stacey shook her head and squeezed Raina's hand.

"You're definitely not alone. Karli is here, and Frannie and I will always be available to you. If you need anything."

"Thanks. I really appreciate that. I wouldn't wish my experiences on anyone, but I'm glad I met you. And I'm glad Karli is back in my life."

"She seems like a really good friend."

Raina smiled. "She is. Not many people would take someone in after so many years, especially someone in my situation. But Karli offered."

"It's good to have people like that in your life."

"Yes, it is. Hey, do you want to stay for dinner? It has to be almost finished."

Stacey stood and shook her head. "No, I don't want to intrude more than I already did."

"It's not an intrusion. Besides, I think Jessica is on her way over. We can make it a girls' night."

Someone knocked on the door. Raina held up a finger and went to the door. She looked through the peephole, then unlocked the door.

"Hello!" Jessica said, hugging Raina as she walked into the apartment. "I brought—Stacey! I didn't know you were going to be here! How are you?"

"I'm trying to convince her to stay for dinner," Raina said.

"Oh, you have to. I brought wine, and we were going to watch Princess Bride." Jessica grinned widely, imploring Stacey with her eyes.

"Oh, fine. I can't say no to the two of you. Thank you for inviting me." Stacey laughed when they hugged her.

"Let me go tell Karli she can stop hiding," Raina said. "You two open the wine."

"On it," Jessica said with a salute. "So, how are you?"

Stacey shrugged. "Not great. I can't deny that staying

here for dinner is more appealing than going home and having my husband not talk to me. Again." She sent Wray a text that she wouldn't be home for dinner and not to wait for her.

"Why isn't he talking to you?"

"I wish I knew. Things were better for a while. I mean, sort of. We were communicating some. But then he got an attitude with me one night and has been back on the couch every night since and barely speaks to me."

"That's weird."

Stacey nodded and accepted the glass of wine Jessica poured her. "It's just hard. I feel like things are so broken between us that I'm not sure we'll ever be able to fix them, but then sometimes it seems like everything is going to be okay."

"That sucks. I'm so sorry."

Stacey waved her hand dismissively. "Thanks. We'll figure it out eventually. How are things going with you? Any progress with Braden?"

"Who's Braden?" Raina asked as she walked back into the living room.

Jessica's cheeks turned pink. "He's my boss's brother."

"Jessica has liked him forever. He's my husband's best friend," Stacey said.

"Oh, that's how you two know each other?" Raina asked.

Stacey and Jessica nodded. "Taylor, Braden's sister, was like a sister to Wray. She invites everyone over from time to time. And she's trying to play matchmaker with Jessica and Braden."

"Except he's never seemed all that interested," Jessica said.

"Who's not interested?" Karli asked, joining the others with a tray of food in each hand.

Stacey's stomach rumbled loudly. She pressed her hand to it and tried not to inhale all the air in the room so she could bring that smell inside herself quicker. "Damn that smells good."

"Thank you," Karli said. "It's an appetizer sampler so we can munch on it all night while we watch the movie and drink and not feel guilty about how much we're eating because it's small portions and those don't count."

Stacey liked Karli even more. All the women were curvy. Stacey often felt ashamed of her figure, but being around women who looked the same made her less conscious of it. And being around women who celebrated their curves made her want to do the same. Karli was celebrating.

Karli set the trays on the coffee table and accepted a glass of wine from Raina. "Who's not interested?" she asked again, looking at Jessica.

"Braden. Taylor's brother. She keeps trying to push us together. We're getting together Friday night, but I don't think it's a date. He's oblivious. Or not interested. Either way, I just don't think it's going to work."

"You didn't tell me you were going out. That's awesome! And you can't give up on someone you've wanted for so long. Especially before it even starts," Karli said.

"How long have you wanted him?" Stacey asked.

"An embarrassingly long time. Years. Since I started working for Taylor." Jessica's cheeks darkened with the admission.

"I know Braden pretty well, and I think he's just unsure of himself. He doesn't see himself as a catch. He's told me more than once he wishes he had what Wray and I have. Or what we used to have." Stacey didn't want to imagine her marriage was over, but she had a hard time hoping things would change again. Even when she and Wray were sleeping together, it was different. There was a distance between them. A block. And she put it there to protect her heart. She was scared to let him all the way in again. To be vulnerable to her husband and be crushed by another betrayal. What would the next one be?

"You and Wray will figure things out," Jessica said softly, drawing Stacey's attention.

Stacey smiled at her. "We'll see."

"Do you love your husband?" Raina asked.

Stacey was surprised by the question. She nodded. "I do."

"Do you trust your husband?" Raina asked.

Stacey sucked in a breath. That was the harder question to answer. "I don't know."

"Well, it sounds like you need to figure that out. I knew I couldn't trust Damon. He was evil. He was manipulative and dangerous. At first, he was charming and sweet. He would spoil me. He was so good at it that I didn't realize he was spoiling me so I'd spend more and more time with him and stop seeing other people. I stopped going out with friends and people from work. Then I would complain that they didn't invite me and I didn't enjoy my job as much, so he talked me into spending more time with him and eventually quitting my job. He said he would take care of me. He took everyone away from me, and then he showed me who he really was. Trusting him meant giving up my entire life, but someone told me in a healthy relationship, trust means expanding your life and making it better." Raina smiled at Stacey as she repeated her words.

"You're right," Stacey said. "And I believe that. Wray isn't evil. He's a good man and a good father. But he made a big mistake. The kind of mistake I'm not sure I can forgive him for."

"Has he apologized?" Karli asked.

Stacey nodded.

"Do you think he's really sorry?" Karli added appetizers to a plate and sat back on the couch.

"I do." Stacey took a plate from Raina and started collecting appetizers for her dinner.

"Do you think he's going to do anything like that again?" Karli closed her eyes on a bite of food and groaned. "Sorry, that's damn good."

Stacey chuckled. "You should love your food. And no. I don't think he'll do anything like what he did. He got in over his head."

"So, you need to decide if you're going to trust the part of you that says he'll never do it again or the part of you that says it's too big to forgive."

Karli's words rolled around in Stacey's head as she ate dinner and watched the movie. She made it sound so simple, but there was nothing simple about deciding if her marriage could be saved.

Stacey left with Jessica, saying goodbye in the private lot for residents and guests before going home. The house was quiet when she walked in, telling her she missed the boys. Stacey tiptoed in, closing the door softly so she didn't disturb Wray. She was almost to the stairs when he finally said the words that she hated to hear.

"We need to talk."

14

———

Stacey stared at him for a long moment. He waited, wondering if she was going to have the conversation or not. If she took off, he would follow her, but he didn't want to have to do that.

She sighed, then turned from the stairs and walked toward him. She moved around the end of the couch and sat in the chair on the opposite side of the room. She folded her hands in her lap and stared at them.

Wray sat down on the couch. A part of him expected her to just spill everything, but if she was going to do that, they wouldn't be sitting across the room from each other in silence.

"Where were you tonight?"

"I was checking on a client. She moved in with a friend and I went to see how she was doing. Jessica showed up, and they invited me to stay and have dinner with them."

"Is that really where you were?"

She looked up at him, her eyes wide. "Why would I lie about that?"

Wray shrugged. "You seem to be avoiding telling me a lot of things lately."

"Like what?"

"Like you're following a man who murdered his wife and is involved in human trafficking."

Stacey gasped. She went still for a minute, not moving or responding.

Wray waited. He didn't want to rush to talk and have her not tell him something. He needed to understand why, and he needed her to understand how dangerous it was.

"I told her she would be safe. I said going back to a life was a good idea."

"This is not your fault."

Her lip wobbled. "It is, though. If I had encouraged her to move, to leave the area, she'd still be alive."

"You don't know that."

"She'd have a better chance. He's evil. He killed her in broad daylight and got away with it."

"Marcus is still looking into it."

"Marcus has nothing. If he could prove anything, he would have Oscar in jail already."

"Why is this one so important to you?" Wray asked. He kept trying to figure out that answer. It was the one thing he didn't understand. All her clients mattered, but she'd never gotten this involved before.

"She has a daughter. I think he might hurt her."

Wray sucked in a sharp breath. He still saw the woman from the fire. Through his entire shift, whenever he closed his eyes, he saw her body. She was small, probably young, but they'd never know for sure.

"Holly sent me a letter. Her neighbor sent it after she died. It said Oscar was following her. He found her. And she said if anything happened to her, she was sure it would be because of him. She asked me to protect her daughter. To get her away from him."

"There was a fire yesterday. At a warehouse," Wray said. "A witness saw a van pull away before the fire, and the van was parked in the same place as the woman's car. Did Marcus talk to you?"

Stacey nodded. "I saw the video of Oscar, but I couldn't say for sure it was him. Frannie watched it, too."

"Did Marcus tell you there was a woman left behind at the fire?"

"What? No, he didn't tell us that."

"It's not really relevant to the video. If Oscar was the one in the video, and if he's the one who moved those women, and if he's the one who started the fire, he's dangerous."

"He killed my client. I already know he's dangerous."

"I know you do, but I don't think you know how dangerous. The body is gone."

"What are you talking about?"

"The woman Braden and I found in the fire? The ME took her body yesterday. They were going to run tests today and try to determine her identity. She's gone. The files, the body, everything. Like she was never there."

"How is that possible?"

"Someone didn't want her to be found. They didn't want anyone to know who she was."

Stacey rubbed her hands up and down her arms and shivered. "That's horrible. Her family will never know."

Wray shook his head. "No, they won't. And I'm afraid the same thing is going to happen to you if you keep following Oscar."

Stacey glared at Wray. "I'm not going to let him get away with what he did."

"And I'm not going to let you get yourself killed and have

your body disposed of God knows where so I never find you. We have sons to think about, Stacey. There are people who love you."

"There were people who loved that woman, who loved Holly. Who knows how many others he took out of that warehouse before it went up in flames. How can you say it's okay for someone like him to be out in the world?"

Wray shook his head. "It's not. I will never think it is. But it's not your job to put him away."

"I can't walk away from this, Wray."

"I can't lose you," he breathed.

She drew a shaky breath and lifted her gaze to his. "I didn't think you cared."

"I love you, Stacey. I always have."

"The last week..."

"Are you having an affair?"

"What?"

Wray leveled her with his gaze. "You were coming home late, leaving early, refusing to tell me what you were doing or who you were with. I told myself that was the only explanation for what was going on."

"I've never cheated on you. I wouldn't."

Wray nodded slowly, trusting the words and thankful she said them. "I believe you, but that's why I've been distant. I couldn't bring myself to ask you and find out we were over, but I couldn't be with you when I believed there was someone else."

"I'm sorry," she whispered. "I didn't want to get you involved or have you worry."

"I'm both now. We reported to both fires yesterday. And I'm always worried about you. Do you think Oscar is the one who threatened you?"

Stacey nodded slowly. "I'm sure of it."

"Stacey, I really don't think you following him is a good idea. He's obviously willing to kill people."

"I am careful. And I'm not backing down from this, Wray. You put yourself in danger all the time."

"I have a team, a partner. I'm not alone. You don't tell me where you're going. You don't tell anyone."

She leaned forward and met his gaze. "What if I tell you? What if I text you my location and promise to check in at a certain time?"

"God, Stacey, I don't know."

She got up from her chair and moved across the room. She sat next to him on the couch and took his hand in hers. "I can't let Vera go through what Holly did. I can't. She's a good kid. Smart and strong, with a bright future. But her father can take that from her. He can destroy her the way he did Holly. It's not fair. Please, let me help her."

"You're going to do it whether I agree or not, aren't you?"

She breathed a laugh and smiled. "I didn't say that."

Wray tugged her against his side and pressed his nose to her hair. "I can't lose you. I won't survive."

"I don't plan on getting lost."

"We usually don't."

"You would survive without me. You'd be a lot busier, but you'd figure it out."

Wray shook his head and squeezed her to his side. "I don't think I would, Stacey. You're everything to me. I love you. Just the idea of losing you makes me want to claw out my insides. When I was... When they took me, and I thought I'd never see you again, it almost broke me. I didn't care that they kicked my ass or threatened to kill me, I hated that I walked out the door that day without telling you how much I love you. And when they brought me back, I couldn't breathe when I saw you. I wasn't sure it would happen, and when it did, it was like I knew everything would be okay."

She looked up at him with tears running down her cheeks. "I was so scared. I was just broken. When you came back, I didn't care where you were or what happened, just that you were home and you were safe. Knowing why you were gone made me mad, but more than that, it terrified me because it could happen again."

"It'll never happen again," Wray said firmly. He cupped her jaw and tilted her face up to his. "I swear on my life I will never let anything like that happen again. I'm done gambling and taking shortcuts."

Stacey nodded. "I know you are. But you could still die at work or driving down the street or when you're out for a run."

"And if I do, I hope you and the boys know I love you. You three are my world. I'm not going to do anything to jeopardize that again. Ever. I want to be here. I will sleep on the couch forever if that's what you want me to do, but I want to be here. Under this roof with the three of you."

Stacey shook her head and stood. She held out her hand for Wray. He put his in hers and let her pull him to his feet. "I think it's time the couch becomes a couch only again."

Her whispery words settled inside him and pulled all the broken pieces of him back together again.

Stacey led the way toward the stairs, pausing to turn off the lights and make sure the door was locked. She held his hand as they tiptoed up the stairs and closed the bedroom door.

Wray tugged her hand before she got too far into their room. She fell into his arms. She tilted her face up, meeting him halfway in a kiss that felt like home.

He wrapped his arms around her waist and pulled her in

close, their bodies touching from lips to hips. They walked together in the darkness toward the bed, tugging at each other's clothes as they went.

She lifted his shirt and spread her hands wide on his chest. She dragged her nails down his abs and wound her hands around his waist to pull him close again.

He unhooked her bra beneath her shirt, circling his hands around to her front to free her breasts. He cupped them, loving the feel of them in his palms. He always loved her breasts, the weight of them and the way it made her crazy when he—

"Oh, God," she moaned against his lips.

He rolled her nipples in his fingers again and flicked his thumb over them. She bucked against him, her body taking over for her muddled mind.

She pulled back from their kiss and struggled to pull her shirt over her head while he continued to play with her nipples. When she finally freed herself, she huffed and yanked her bra off, tossing it to the side.

"Wray," she whispered, part moan, part plea.

"What do you need, Stace?"

"You. Just you. Please."

"Always. I'm always here for you."

He reluctantly released her breasts and tugged his shirt off. She took advantage of the moment and stripped her pants and panties off, stepping out of them and climbing onto the bed.

Wray stared at his wife and thanked God he was so damn lucky. He yanked off his pants and briefs and kicked them to the side before he prowled toward her.

She scooted up the bed and away from him, smiling as he moved closer. Wray leaned over her, only letting their lips touch when he sealed his mouth to hers.

She moaned in his mouth, pushing her tongue inside. He held himself above her, showing her how much he wanted her with his kiss.

Stacey reached down and wrapped her hand around his erection. Wray jerked at the contact, already too close. He'd been beating himself up for a week about his wife having an affair, and knowing she was still his made him desperate to pick up where they left off.

She stroked him once, squeezing as she moved toward his head, then swiping her thumb over his tip.

He groaned and gave up on supporting his body weight, laying down next to her on the bed so he could use his hands, too. She stroked him as he gently caressed her breasts. Her steady strokes faltered, then resumed their rhythm when he moved on. Until he settled his fingers between her thighs.

She was wet, dripping down her thighs. He groaned at the feel of her and pushed himself up. He had to taste her. Her hand felt like heaven, but her pussy was heaven, and he wasn't going to wait.

Stacey moaned at the first swipe of his tongue through her folds. He pressed her thighs wide, opening her up and spearing his tongue inside her. She whimpered and fucked his face, thrusting her hips against his tongue with each plunge.

Wray suckled her soft skin, making quick work of the path between her entrance and her clit. He pressed a finger inside and flattened his tongue to her clit. She lifted her hips, rolling them against his face. He drew back and added a second finger, not giving her time to adjust to him. He needed her. They needed each other.

She moaned when he slid both fingers into her. He flicked her clit with his tongue and sucked on it. He pumped his fingers in and out, loving the way her body responded to him. Her channel rippled around his fingers, drawing him in and tightening around him with each press inside.

Wray could tell she was getting close and reached up with his free hand to her breast. He squeezed it tight, then rasped his fingers over her nipple like his tongue over her clit. Her entire body tightened, and she seemed to stop breathing. Then everything let go.

She panted out her breath and moaned out her release. She pressed her hips to his hands, fucking his fingers back with eagerness. She cupped his head and pressed his face against her core, riding out the waves of her orgasm as he sucked her up into another one and licked her body on the way down.

Everything inside her finally relaxed, and her hands fell to her sides. Wray sucked his fingers clean, loving the taste of his wife. She spread her thighs wide for him as he repositioned himself to kneel.

"God, I love you," she whispered.

"I hope you love me for more than just sex."

She shook her head. "That was not just sex. That was amazing, mind-blowing, soul-searching sex."

"I'm just an orgasm machine for you?" he asked with a smirk.

"If I could put all of that into a vibrator, I might not need you." She paused and smiled up at him. "But I'll always want you."

Wray drew a breath, her words hitting him hard. That was what he'd been missing the last few months. It was that little thing that he needed to know. That he needed to hear. It wasn't that she still loved him. It was that she still wanted him. More than anything, that told him they were going to be okay.

"I'll always want you, too," Wray said, his voice rough with emotion.

She cupped his jaw and pulled him down on top of her. She kissed him gently. He was careful to not deepen the kiss, but she parted her lips and tasted herself on his. He kissed her back, needing that shared connection. Needing that moment when it was all going to be okay.

Stacey shifted her hips until their bodies were lined up. Her heat called to him, and he adjusted until he could dip inside her. They kept kissing while he thrust into her with short strokes, strokes that were not nearly enough.

He pulled back from their kiss and pushed himself up. He lined himself up and slowly pressed inside his wife. Their gazes locked and held. All the pain of the last few months drifting away like a lost balloon.

Wray needed slow. He needed Stacey, but he needed slow. He needed to stay inside her as long as possible. A slow glide in, then an easy retreat. Over and over with their gazes connected. He watched when her eyes widened as an orgasm started to blossom inside her. He loved when she drew her lip between her teeth. He surprised her with a hard thrust in that almost sent her over the edge.

Then he slowed down again. Steady, deep strokes carried them both higher together. The slippery feel of her body coating his and the two of them coming together sent his head into a spiral of need and want and love.

Stacey was it for him. She always had been, but after almost losing her, he knew he had forever. He knew she was his forever.

His orgasm started with a tingle in the back of his throat. Subtle, but insistent. His thrusts carried more force, and Stacey met his strokes. They stared at each other and rose together, watching each other as they fell at the same time.

She pulsed around him as he throbbed inside her. Sex was always good, but he'd never felt that kind of connection with her before. It was stronger, better.

He hated what they went through, but he knew everything happened for a reason. Maybe they needed to go through it in order to find their way back together in this new place.

All Wray knew was he never wanted to leave. He was home.

15

Stacey knew her time to figure out what was going on with Oscar was running out. She had to get justice for Holly, or she was going to end up having to give up. Wray wouldn't let her do this forever, and she didn't want to. She wanted to protect Vera and get her away from her father. It was time to make that happen.

Two days after Wray moved back into their bedroom for good, Stacey waited outside Oscar's house. She watched as Vera left for school, walking with her head down. Stacey ached for the girl and made her a silent promise she'd fix everything soon.

It took an hour, but Oscar finally left. Stacey was still driving her rental car, and she tied her hair up in a bun. She knew it was still possible to figure out who she was, but she was doing everything she could to make sure Oscar didn't see her.

He drove through the city and ended up on the east side. He pulled up to a small warehouse and honked. A roll-up door lifted, and he drove inside.

Stacey debated what to do. She wanted to find some kind of proof of what Oscar was involved in, but she couldn't walk up there and knock on the door and ask. She had to be smart. Clever. A vigilante.

She tucked her keys into the pocket of her leggings and sent Wray a text with her location. She promised to be in touch in thirty minutes. Then she put on the mask Frannie gave her and got out of her car.

The area around the warehouse was pretty dead. There were other buildings nearby, but there weren't a lot of cars. Stacey's heart pounded as she moved around one of the buildings and came up to a dirty window on the side of the building Oscar disappeared into.

The bottom edge of the window was waist high and towered above the ground. Stacey wasn't sure if she could get inside, but she hadn't come so far to give up.

A quick peek told Stacey there were no lights on inside whatever room the window led into. She pressed her ear to the glass and heard no sounds. She had to try.

It didn't take much for the window to lift away from the building. The arm that supported it as Stacey lifted it didn't give her curvy body much space, but it was enough to squeeze between the window frame and the window. She checked inside and found the room, some kind of office, blissfully empty.

She sat on the edge of the frame and pulled her knees up until she could clear the arm holding the window open. She stood on tiptoes and silently lowered herself into the room. She debated leaving the window open, but she didn't want to risk someone realizing she was in the building.

Stacey moved across the room, looking around as she went. The daylight outside provided her with enough light to see the office hadn't been in use in years. A layer of dust coated every horizontal surface. A chair was on its side and a file cabinet stood in the corner, all the drawers open and empty. The cheap, standard desk had a cracked plastic desktop sorter on top and a keyboard pad, but no keyboard.

Stacey walked quietly to the open door to the office, listening for any sounds louder than her pounding heart. Muffled voices met her ears when she reached the door, keeping her in the office.

She strained to make out what they were saying. One of the voices could have been Oscar's, but she wasn't close enough to hear them.

Stacey peeked into the hallway and was happy to see it was empty. She stepped out and heard the voices coming from the right, so she headed that direction.

As she got closer, she was able to hear their conversation. Her phone buzzed in her pocket, reminding her that she was on a clock. She needed to get out of there or Wray would come after her.

Stacey found another empty office, one that was close enough to hear the conversation happening nearby. She hid behind the open door and prayed no one would find her there.

"We have to move everything. It's been sitting here too long," the man said.

"It'll be fine. No one's come looking. The cops don't know about this place." That was definitely Oscar's voice. She pulled out her phone and hit record, hoping it picked up their voices clearly.

"It doesn't matter. You know they won't like it if we leave stuff too long."

"Ugh, I don't get it. Why can't we just do things the way

we think they should be done? We're always moving stuff around the city."

"They make the rules. We just have to do as we're asked."

"Yeah, well, one day, we'll be in charge."

"Do you even know who's in charge?"

"Of course. Don't you?" Oscar's trademark cockiness made Stacey roll her eyes. If she had to guess, he didn't know anything.

"No. I just pick up whatever they tell me when they tell me. I had to do a run of drugs last week."

"That's nothing. I had to get a bunch of women. They smelled like ass. And not the good kind either."

"There's a good kind of ass?" the guy asked with a chuckle.

"Yeah, ass that's being handled. You couldn't pay me to fuck any of those women. If I wasn't supposed to burn the van, I would have anyway. No way to get a smell like that out."

"I'm glad I didn't have to do that. Guns are easier. They don't talk back."

Oscar laughed loudly, the sudden sound scaring Stacey. She lost her balance and slipped, falling onto her backside.

She froze, wondering if they heard her.

"Did you hear that?" the other guy asked.

"Hear what?" Oscar asked.

"Sounded like someone is in the building."

"We'd know. Come on. Let's get these guns loaded up so they can pay us. We have a lot of work to do."

Stacey didn't move until their voices grew quieter. When she was sure they were gone, she eased to her feet. She took her time, moving painfully slowly back to the office she used to get inside the building. When she was sure they weren't around, she pushed the window open and let herself out the way she came in.

She walked around the building next door and made her way back to her rental car with her heart pounding against her chest. She could barely breathe. She locked the door and started the car, pulling away from the side of the road without bothering with her seatbelt.

Only when she was back in the city did she finally start to feel like she was going to be okay. She didn't think anyone followed her, and she finally had proof that Oscar was involved in something illegal. Guns, drugs, and women. The bad guy trifecta.

Stacey called Wray when her hands were no longer shaking, surprised it had only been twenty-seven minutes since she sent him the text. He answered on the first ring.

"Stacey? Are you okay? Where are you?"

"I'm fine. I'm okay. I promise. I followed Oscar, and I heard a conversation he had with another man. They're moving guns right now."

"Guns? Are you serious?"

"I am. I recorded their conversation. Part of it, at least. They were talking about moving guns right now, but women and drugs before. And Oscar mentioned the van and the women and the fire."

"Jesus." Wray was silent for a minute. "He didn't see you?"

"No. I stayed out of sight. I hid in an office. But I have to talk to Marcus. I have to give him this recording."

"Are you going there now?"

"I am. I have an appointment this afternoon with a client, but I told Frannie I was taking the morning off."

"Do you want me to meet you at the police station?"

"No. Thank you, though. I'm good. I'll call you after I talk to Marcus."

"Okay, good. And Stacey?"

"Yeah?"

"Thank you for letting me know where you were. I love you."

"I love you, too."

She hung up and turned into the police station parking lot. She tucked the mask in her purse and slung the bag over her shoulder, making sure her phone was inside.

Stacey asked at the desk if she could see Captain Patrick and gave her name. The man behind the desk asked her to wait while he called.

Marcus came out a few minutes later. He waved to the desk attendant and waited for Stacey to join him before walking back to his office.

Only when they were closed in his office did Marcus ask why she was there. "I'm assuming this isn't a social call."

Stacey shook her head. "I have something you need to listen to."

Marcus crossed his arms over his chest and raised a brow.

Stacey played the recording, smiling when the voices were clear.

When the recording was over, Stacey waited for Marcus to thank her, but he didn't look as happy as she'd expected.

"Who was that?"

"One voice was Oscar Hyatt. I'm not sure who the other man was."

"Where did you get this?"

"I followed him this morning. They were in a warehouse on the east side of the city. I snuck in and recorded this."

"You could have gotten yourself killed!"

"I'm fine. They didn't see me."

"It sounds like you were lucky. Did you fall?"

Stacey's cheeks heated. "It startled me when he laughed. But they didn't even look for me. They just left."

Marcus grimaced and shook his head. "You know I can't use this, right?"

"What are you talking about?"

"This was an illegal recording. You didn't have their permission to record them, so it's not something I can use to get a warrant."

"If I had their permission, they wouldn't have admitted all of that!" Stacey couldn't believe what he was saying.

"I know, but that's the way the law works. The only thing I can act on is if I receive a tip from a confidential informant that someone is in a warehouse on the east side and moving guns. That's something I can use to send a team out to see what's going on."

"Then do that," Stacey said. "Do something. You can't let him get away with anything else. You heard him confess to moving those women and burning the van."

"This won't put him away for Holly's murder," Marcus said gently.

Stacey sighed. "I know. But it'll protect Vera from him."

"Are you sure you want to do that? You want her to go into the system?"

"She has an aunt somewhere in Illinois. Holly talked about going there to start over, but liked this area. She wanted as much stability for Vera as possible."

"And you think disrupting that is for the best?"

"Marcus, they are trafficking women. This is bigger than Holly or Vera. I want to keep Vera safe, and I believe there's a chance Oscar would sell his own daughter, or that they'd take her if he messed up. But regardless of Vera, he needs to be stopped. Whoever he's involved with needs to be stopped. Those women deserve a life."

Marcus thought for a minute, then nodded. "Okay. I'll get a team over there."

Stacey stopped him with a hand on his arm. "Were you really going to let him get away with this?"

Marcus shook his head. "Not a chance. But I needed to know how ready you were for whatever the consequences were. I needed you to be prepared for whatever is going to happen to Vera."

Stacey nodded. "Thank you."

Marcus squeezed her bicep. "Thank you for the tip."

Marcus told four officers to meet him in the conference room in a minute, then walked Stacey to the front. She thanked him again for helping and wished him good luck taking down Oscar and whoever else he was involved with.

OSCAR DROPPED off the last of the guns and headed to the warehouse to see Damon. He was hoping he'd get another job to do since the distribution went so smoothly.

Damon was sitting behind his desk, glaring, when Oscar walked in. "Did everything go well?"

"Yep. Perfect. All where they need to be."

"It's lucky you and Antonio got the guns out when you did since the building was raided a few hours after you left."

Oscar nodded. Lucky was his middle name. He hadn't had a loss since he found Holly again. He got rid of her, got his kid back, and was kicking ass at work. He was riding high. Nothing was going to stop him.

"Any idea how that happened?"

"The raid? No. How would I know?"

"Were you followed?"

"I would have known if I was being followed."

"Like you knew all the other times you were being followed?"

The way Damon said it sent a chill up Oscar's spine. Was it possible Damon had him followed? And that Oscar didn't notice?

"I checked. That woman hasn't come after me since I threatened her. She knows I won't back down. I'll kill her if I have to."

"And that's the best way to handle a threat?"

"Sure. Why not?"

Damon nodded slowly. His index fingers were steepled in front of his face, tapping on his lips. He slid his elbows across the desk and unfolded his hands. "I have a new job for you."

Oscar smiled, nodding as Damon reached into a desk drawer and pulled out a folder.

"I need a debt collected. The man who owes me has been stealing from me. He thinks I don't know it, but I've been keeping track. I would like you to pay him a visit and get what he owes me."

"What if he doesn't have it?" Oscar asked.

"You have my permission to get creative."

Oscar raised his brows. He'd never been given an open-ended assignment before. "What does that mean?"

"It means take it from him in whatever way you need to. If he has a wife or a daughter, you can take one of them. If he has valuables, you can take those. If he has none of the above, you can take it from him."

Oscar swallowed. Holly was the first and only person he'd killed. He'd had his share of fights, but he didn't get the idea this one would be fair.

"Oh, and I want you to take Antonio with you."

"Antonio? Why?"

"Because the man who owes me is his father."

"But won't he try to help his father?"

"If he does, kill him, too."

"You want me to kill the man?"

"You said the best way to handle a threat is to kill them. This man poses a threat. He's been stealing from me. He isn't being honest. He's threatening the Company. And I'm not willing to sit back and allow it to continue."

Oscar wasn't sure what to say. He didn't plan to kill Holly when he did. He was angry that she embarrassed him. That she made him look like a fool. When he dragged her out of her car, he was just going to rough her up. Remind her that he was the man and he was in charge.

But she fought back. She was stronger than before. She didn't cower in fear and take it. She even got a few good hits in herself.

That was when he pulled out the knife. The first stab slowed her down. The second one made her gasp. But the third one Oscar actually enjoyed. It was like hitting her for the first time again. The surprise in her eyes. The fear. He got hard when he saw that fear. And he kept going. When she sank to the sidewalk and stopped fighting him, he realized what he did.

He wasn't a cold-blooded killer. Showing an old man he meant business was one thing, but killing him was another. Oscar wasn't sure he had it in him to do it.

"Is there a problem?" Damon asked, his voice sharp as a blade.

Oscar shook his head. "No, sir. Of course not. Antonio and I will go over there tonight. I'll let you know how it goes."

"Good. I hope to see you back here with my money and no blood on your hands, but I'll take whatever you bring me."

Oscar's gut flipped as he considered the rest of his night. This was not the kind of job he hoped to get. But he had no choice. He was in now. And there were only two ways out.

And neither included saying no to the boss.

16

Stacey rolled over in bed and reached blindly for her ringing phone. The buzz and beep alternated, irritating her more and more with each second that she couldn't find the offending item on her nightstand.

Finally, she wrapped her hand around the vibrating phone and swiped to answer the call without bothering to look at who it was. She never knew the number when she was on call, anyway. It was always blocked or a pay phone or some other call that didn't really matter where it came from. Someone needed help.

"Hello?" Stacey groaned, trying not to sound like she'd just been woken from a dead sleep.

"Stacey?" The timid voice on the other end shook.

Stacey sat bolt upright. "Yeah?" She knew the voice, but identifying it when she was barely able to remember her own name and answer in agreement of that question was beyond her capabilities.

"Stacey, it's Vera. I need you. Can you help me?"

Stacey tossed the covers aside as soon as the girl said her

name. She snatched a discarded pair of jeans from the chair in the corner and went to the closet to find a bra and shirt.

"Of course, Vera. Where are you?"

"I'm at the police station."

"What? Why? What happened? Are you okay?"

She sniffed, and her next words were gummy, like they were said through tears. "They're looking for my dad."

"I'm on my way, honey. I will be there soon."

"Okay." Vera hung up, giving Stacey a second to take a deep breath.

"What's going on?" Wray asked. He was sitting up in bed. His chest was bare, his hair mussed, his eyes glazed and sleepy.

"Vera is at the police station. She said they're looking for her dad."

"What does that mean?"

Stacey shook her head. "I have no idea, but I'm going to find out. I knew she wasn't safe with him."

"Are you going to take her to Shelter?"

"Probably. I know she's safe there. And it's an approved center for displaced kids, so she can stay without it being an issue. For now, at least."

"Do you need me to do anything?"

"No. Just stay here with the boys. It might be a long night for me."

Stacey walked over to Wray's side of the bed and leaned over to kiss him. He returned the quick kiss with a quick inhale and grabbed her hand. "Promise me you won't go after him."

She tilted her head to the side and closed her eyes. "I don't know if I can do that."

"Then promise me you'll let me know where you're

going if you go anywhere other than the police station and Shelter."

"I might need to take Vera home to get some clothes."

"Stacey, please. I know this is important to you. But you're important to me."

She hesitated for a minute, then nodded. She didn't want him to get in trouble or be in danger, but she knew whatever Oscar was involved in was bigger than any of them. It wouldn't take much for Stacey to be in over her head.

"I love you," Wray said.

"I love you." She leaned down and kissed him once more, then left for the police station.

She was in her car before Stacey realized it was almost three in the morning. Her mind whirred with possibilities for why Vera was at the police station and why they were looking for Oscar. Stacey had a lot of theories, but the only thing that mattered was the truth.

The police station was quiet in the middle of the night. She gave them her name and told them why she was there. She was led back to a room and questioned since she was asking to see a minor in police custody.

"Can I ask why she's here?" Stacey questioned the officer once she proved her identity and place of employment.

"We got a call about an attack earlier tonight. Two men were assaulted, one dead and one alive. When we got there, the guy named the girl's father as the person who attacked them. We went to his home address and found the girl there alone. She said she didn't know where her father was. Didn't even realize he wasn't home. She was scared, so we brought her here until she could go somewhere safe."

"Do you know who the men were? That he assaulted?"

The officer's face turned to stone. "I can't comment on active investigations, ma'am."

Stacey nodded and didn't push. She'd get everything out of Marcus. "Can I see Vera now?"

The officer led the way down another hallway. At the end was a room with blinds drawn low over windows. Inside was Vera, curled up on a couch under a blanket with a mug of something steaming.

"Stacey," she shouted, setting the mug on the coffee table with a loud thunk. She rushed across the room to Stacey and threw herself in her arms. And cried.

The officer nodded at Stacey and pulled the door closed behind himself as he walked out. Stacey held Vera and tried to soothe her as the girl sobbed. Her entire body shook, the tears coming from a depth she likely hadn't found before.

Stacey brushed Vera's blonde locks back from her face and hated the pain she saw. Vera's face scrunched up like she hadn't ever been so hurt or scared before in her life. Vera was strong, like her mother, but Stacey guessed she hadn't been able to cry for her mother after she died, and now she could lose her father, too.

They moved to the couch where Vera was sitting when Stacey walked in. Vera's sobs turned to hiccups. She wiped at her tears, her pale skin splotchy from crying. Her emerald eyes shined with the leftover tears. Dots soaked into the gray sweatshirt she wore, blending with spots there from an earlier crying session if Stacey had to guess.

"Are you okay? Are they taking care of you?" Stacey asked.

Vera nodded, chewing her lip. She tugged on the string from the sweatshirt and stared at the coffee table.

"What happened, honey?"

Vera's lip wobbled when she looked up at Stacey. "Am I in trouble?"

"What? No. Of course not. Why would you think that?"

She shrugged. "They said my dad did something bad."

"Everyone is innocent until proven guilty," Stacey reminded the teenager. There was little doubt in Stacey's mind that Oscar did exactly what he was accused of, but she wasn't going to share that with his daughter.

"He's not a good man. If he would hurt my mom the way he did, he would hurt others." Vera looked up at Stacey and leveled her with a look that was far older than a fourteen-year-old should have. "Did he kill my mom?"

Stacey wasn't sure how to answer the question. She believed it was likely, but she had no proof. Neither did the cops. She couldn't tell Vera he didn't, not with any certainty, but saying she thought he did wouldn't keep her safe either.

"I don't know," Stacey finally said. "The evidence says no, but…"

"He was following her. Did you know that?"

"How do you know that?"

"I saw him. I asked my mom if it was him, and she said no, but I know it was. It was him. And I think he killed her."

"We don't know that, honey. We have no proof."

"But they have proof this time. About whatever he did."

Stacey drew in a breath. "There's a witness, but that doesn't always mean the witness is telling the truth."

"You don't think he did it?" The hope in Vera's eyes almost broke Stacey's heart. The kid wanted to believe her father was a good man. What kid wouldn't? If Stacey shattered that, she didn't know what would happen.

"I don't know. I don't know anything about what's going on. But Marcus will know."

"He doesn't like me," Vera said, pulling back into herself.

She sat back on the couch and brought her knees up, wrapping her hands around them.

"I don't think that's true. Marcus is hard to get to know. He has a tendency to keep to himself."

"Either way, he won't tell me anything."

"If he can, he will. Are you okay staying at Shelter for a while? Until the police can figure out what's going on with your dad?"

Vera nodded.

Stacey could see the exhaustion settling in on the girl. She stood and looked around for a bag or something with Vera's clothes. "Do you have clothes?"

Vera stood and shook her head. "They didn't even let me bring my phone."

"Do you want to go home and get some stuff?"

"Am I allowed?"

"We'll ask. Maybe someone can go with us."

ONE OF THE cops on duty took Vera and Stacey to Vera's house in the police car. He parked on the street, blocking the driveway. He turned off the vehicle and escorted them to the door. He walked in first, ducking below the police tape across the front door.

Stacey noticed the frame was splintered from where the door was smashed in. Her heart ached for Vera, home alone and hearing that sound.

The officer checked the house and said it was safe for them to move around. He let himself back out and asked for them to be out in ten minutes.

Stacey followed Vera to her bedroom. Vera stopped at the door, then drew a breath and walked into her room.

"Do you need some help?" Stacey offered.

Vera shook her head. "I'm just going to grab stuff for a few days. I can always come back if I need to. Maybe. I guess I don't know."

"I think we can make that happen if you end up staying longer," Stacey said. "Do you have a suitcase or something?" When Vera and Holly arrived at the shelter, their belongings were packed in black trash bags slung over their shoulders. Anything that wouldn't be noticed when they left Oscar.

"The suitcase is in my dad's room. Will you get it? It's across the hall."

Stacey nodded and left Vera to gather her things. She turned on the light in the other bedroom and stepped inside. The room was dark, with paneled walls and dim lighting. The unmade bed was a metal frame with no head-board or footboard. Three pillows were tossed around like they were flipped while someone was looking for something.

Looking for something?

Stacey checked behind her for Vera. She was staring at her dresser, sorting through clothes to take with her.

Stacey turned back to the messy room. Was there anything there? Anything that could prove Oscar killed Holly?

Nothing stood out, but Stacey didn't expect to find a box marked *evidence*. She opened the drawers to his nightstand and closed them again quickly when she found condoms and a phone charger. She opened each of his four dresser drawers, but all she found were clothes.

The closet made sense for where the suitcase was, so it wasn't like she was snooping when she opened it. Clothes hung off bent metal hangers. Shoes tangled and toppled together on the floor. On the one shelf above the small hanging bar was a suitcase that was taped together and didn't look like it would actually keep things inside.

Stacey pulled it down with ease. She was disappointed to see there was nothing else on the top shelf. She wanted proof.

"You found it. I think I have everything I want to bring," Vera said from the doorway.

Stacey smiled over at her and nodded. She cast one last glance around the room and followed Vera back to her room to pack up her stuff.

"I wasn't sure if I should bring stuff for school or just to relax. I don't know what to do. Last time, Mom was with me."

Stacey hugged Vera to her side. She wished she could make the whole thing easier for her, but no matter what happened, it wasn't going to be easy.

"We'll figure it out together."

Vera smiled and put the suitcase on her bed. She started shoving clothes into it, not bothering to organize them in the slightest. When her bed was empty and the suitcase was full, Vera leaned across it to tug the zipper closed and a necklace swung free from her sweatshirt.

It caught the light and sparkled. Stacey stared at it, wondering if she could somehow be mistaken.

"Vera, where did you get that necklace? Did your mom give it to you?"

Vera finished zipping the suitcase and shook her head. She clasped the bird and lifted it with a smile. "No. But it's just like mom's. Dad said he found it at a store and wanted me to have something to remember her by."

Ice ran through Stacey's veins. "Yeah? Your mom's had an engraving on it. Does this one have the same?"

Vera laughed softly. "It does. The same exact one." She

looked up at Stacey with a smile. "It's how I know my dad is a good guy. I mean, if he wasn't, he wouldn't have given me something so special. Something that's exactly like my mom's, so I always know she's with me. So I always know to *Fly Free*, like it says."

Stacey's heart skipped at the words. She forced a smile for Vera, but Oscar's story was a lie. The necklace was custom made, one of a kind. It wasn't something you could walk into a store and buy. Taylor had it made just for Holly, and she added the inscription on the back to help inspire her. The only way Oscar could have the necklace was if he took it off Holly's body when he killed her.

Stacey told the police Holly always wore the necklace, but since Stacey hadn't seen Holly that morning, she couldn't say with absolute certainty Holly was wearing it the day she died.

Now she knew.

"We should go," Stacey said, her body tight with anger. Vera's eyes drooped, anyway. They needed to get to Shelter in the Storm.

The police officer drove them back to the station to get Stacey's vehicle, then followed them to Shelter. Vera was asleep when they got to the shelter. Stacey gently woke her, then let them in the back door, silencing the alarm before it woke everyone else up. Stacey led Vera upstairs to one of the open rooms. Vera curled up on the bed and was asleep before Stacey closed the door and went to find Frannie.

Frannie was already in the kitchen with coffee on and muffins on the table when Stacey walked in.

"Sorry I woke you."

"I figured if you were sneaking in at this hour, it wasn't good."

"It's Vera."

"Vera?" Frannie gasped. "What happened?"

"Two men were assaulted last night. One was still alive when the police arrived and said Oscar did it. They went to his house and found Vera asleep and alone. Took her to the station and let her call me."

"Oh, the poor thing. Did you get her settled?"

Stacey nodded. "Yeah. She probably needs sleep more than anything right now."

Frannie poured two cups of coffee and carried them to the table. "And what do you need?"

"Oscar killed Holly."

Frannie sighed. "I know we think that, but we don't have—"

"Proof? What about the necklace? The custom-made, one-of-a-kind necklace Taylor gave her?"

Frannie's brows tugged together. She tilted her head to the side, her brown hair tumbling over her shoulders. "They never found her necklace."

Stacey nodded. "I found it tonight. Vera's wearing it."

"What?"

"Oscar gave it to her. Said he found it in a store and had them put the same engraving as Holly's. Wanted her to have something that would remind her that her mom is always with her."

"That sick bastard."

Stacey nodded. "That's the proof we need."

"It's more than we had, but I'm not sure it'll be enough."

"It's a start."

Frannie nodded and sipped her coffee. The two of them sat in silence and ate muffins and drank coffee while the shelter started to wake up around them.

Frannie told Stacey to go home and shower and get

some rest before she came back for the day. She promised to call if anything happened with Vera.

Stacey was reluctant, but she knew it was for the best if she took a shower and cleared her head for a minute. She got in her car and was about to call Wray when her phone buzzed.

Except it wasn't her phone.

Stacey looked around and finally found a phone wedged between the passenger seat and the center console.

Vera's phone.

There were multiple texts and calls. Stacey swiped up to see if anything was important, and the phone opened.

Stacey paused. It was a violation of Vera's privacy, but...

She clicked over to her Find My Friends app. Oscar's name was there. And so was his location.

17

———

Stacey followed the dot on the screen, pausing every so often to make sure she was still headed in the right direction. Her heart raced and her palms slipped on the steering wheel. She'd never been so nervous in her entire life. Not when she got married, not when she had the boys, not even when she interviewed for her job at Shelter in the Storm.

None of those were life and death.

She finally got close to where the dot was on the map and pulled over. Her heart was pounding so hard she couldn't hear anything outside her body. She looked around at where she was, surprised to not recognize the area.

Large buildings surrounded her. Signs on some of them indicated the businesses were geared more toward other businesses instead of consumers. A wood shop was across the street, an auto parts supplier in front of her, and a metal fabrication shop at the end of the block.

Stacey knew Oscar was close. The dot was on the backside of the metal fabrication building. Close to the Niagara River.

For a full minute, Stacey sat in her car and tried to take

deep breaths. She was exhausted from being up most of the night with Vera, but she wasn't willing to walk away from Oscar. Not when she knew where he was.

She picked up her phone and dialed Wray. She wanted to update him on Vera. And she owed him the truth about where she was.

He answered on the first ring. "Hey. How's everything going?"

"Vera is safe. She's scared and overwhelmed and confused. She thought her father was a good guy and convinced herself maybe he hadn't killed her mom, but now she's doubting that."

"I'm sorry to hear that. Unfortunately, she's going to learn the truth one day."

"Yeah. She just wasn't prepared for it to be today. It's going to get worse for her."

"Why? What else happened?"

"I found him," Stacey breathed.

"You found who?"

"Oscar. Vera left her phone in my car, and it's tracking him. I'm sitting outside the building where he's hiding right now."

"What?" Wray barked.

Stacey's excitement dimmed at the tone of his voice. "I can't let him get away with this. He gave Vera a necklace that was Holly's."

"Okay?"

"He told her it was like her mom's. That he found it and wanted her to have something that reminded her of her mom. But the necklace Holly had was the only one. Taylor made it for Holly. It's not possible that Oscar bought another one. It's the same one."

"Are you sure?"

"Yes. It has the same inscription and everything. The only way he could have gotten it is if he took it off her after he killed her."

"That sounds like a really stupid thing to do."

Stacey breathed a laugh. "I never said he was smart."

Wray exhaled loudly. "Stace, I don't like you going after this guy. You should call Marcus."

"I will. But first I need to make sure he's here. I need to make sure he's not going to get away this time. Holly..." Stacey paused as emotion filled her throat and lungs. "Holly was a good person. She was kind and caring. She was an amazing mom. Things weren't always bad between her and Oscar. She tried to make it better, but he's evil. He stole her from the world. She had so much to give, and he stole it."

"I know, but—"

"Wray, I can't. I can't sit back on this one. I can't let him go. I have to find him and make sure he goes down for this. I have to."

Wray was silent for a long minute. Stacey didn't breathe while she waited for him to say something. Anything. She knew she was putting herself at risk, her kids and him, but she knew it was the right thing to do. That she had no choice but to make sure the man paid for what he did.

"Text me the address. If I don't hear back from you in twenty minutes, I'm calling Marcus and we're both coming to get you."

Stacey exhaled fully, collapsing over the steering wheel. She didn't realize until that moment how much his approval meant to her. Having him trust her gave her the last little bit of courage she needed to walk inside and face Oscar. To take him down for good.

"Thank you. I... This means a lot."

"Be careful. I love you."

"I love you, too."

Stacey hung up and immediately sent Wray a text with the address. She grabbed her mask from her bag and slid it on, knowing she could do this. She could stop Oscar once and for all.

OSCAR STAYED in the shadows all night, avoiding anywhere that could have a camera or nosy people who thought they were doing the right thing. He was not going down for this. Not when he was ordered to kill that man. It wasn't his fault the guy was still alive. Oscar did his job, dammit. He thought the guy was dead. But with sirens blaring, he didn't have time to stick around and make sure.

Antonio flipped the fuck out when he realized what Oscar was doing. He went after Oscar, breaking his nose before Oscar pulled a knife on the asshole. Antonio tried to fight his way out, but Oscar knew it was kill or be killed. Killing Antonio wasn't part of the plan, but plans didn't matter at that point.

When Oscar finally heard back from Damon with an address to meet, he nearly peed himself in relief. His house was not an option. His job wasn't either. Hell, he couldn't even walk into a store and wash the blood off his face. He needed solace. Somewhere to pull himself together.

The address led to a warehouse a few blocks from where Oscar usually met with Damon. The sign above the door said it was a metal fab company. Oscar followed the instructions to go around to the back and opened the third door.

It was dark inside. The brightness of the day made it

impossible for Oscar to see anything in the building, but he knew Damon wouldn't lead him wrong. Oscar stepped inside and let the door close behind him. He waited for his eyes to adjust, then looked around the small office.

The workshop beyond the office was dimly lit with light from outside filtering through dirty windows and skylights. The office itself was neat, but it was simple, with a single desk and computer, a chair, and a small filing cabinet.

Oscar wasn't sure what he was supposed to do, so he stood there and waited. It felt like forever, but after a minute, he heard voices approaching.

Oscar looked around for somewhere to hide. He wasn't sure whose office it was and didn't want to be caught in there by anyone other than Damon.

Before he could figure out what to do, the door to the workshop swung open and Damon stepped inside. He nodded to the men he'd been speaking to and closed the door, then turned to Oscar.

Oscar swallowed roughly.

"You fucked things up again."

"I thought the man was dead."

"Well, you were wrong."

Oscar nodded. He hadn't slept in twenty-four hours. He was tired, dirty, and frustrated. And he was on the run. He had no patience for Damon.

"I never should have been given that job."

"I needed to know what you were capable of. Now I know."

"It wouldn't have been a big deal if Antonio wasn't there."

"That man wasn't Antonio's father."

"What?" Oscar breathed. "Why the fuck did you tell me he was?"

Damon crossed the room and was in Oscar's face before he could take another breath. "Don't you dare speak to me that way."

Oscar ducked his head. "I'm sorry."

Damon took a step back. "I needed to know if you could handle this job. If either of you could. It turns out you can't."

"Yes, I can," Oscar argued.

Damon shook his head and moved to the desk. He sat down in the chair and pulled on a pair of gloves. Then he clicked a key on the computer to bring it to life.

"Whose office is this?" Oscar asked.

"It's yours."

"What?"

"It's yours. You accepted a job here last week."

"I don't even know what this place is."

"That doesn't really matter. It's just the place you're going to die. After you write your suicide note on your computer and confess all your sins to the world."

"You're fucking nuts," Oscar blurted.

"You're not the first person to have told me so. And I'm sure you won't be the last. It's probably the truth, but none of that matters because it's time for you to take a seat."

Oscar shook his head even as Damon moved around the desk toward him. He had a life. A daughter. Damon was supposed to help him.

"Don't make this harder than it has to be," Damon said softly. "Just sit down at the desk and confess all your sins. Do this for your daughter, so she knows she's better off without you. Because either you're going to do this or I will, but either way, you're not walking out of this room." Damon's eyes turned deadly, and his voice hardened.

Oscar backed away from him. He always knew Damon was the kind of man who commanded respect and admiration, but he didn't see the vicious side of him until that moment. The side that told Oscar he'd never see his daughter again.

He dropped to his knees and started to cry.

STACEY PRESSED herself against the wall as she got closer to the door. She needed to make sure Oscar was inside, then she'd get the hell out and call for help. Let the police take him down.

Unless she had a chance to talk to him. She wanted to make sure he knew that she was the one who figured it all out. That Holly helped. That he wasn't going to get away with anything.

Stacey gripped the cold metal handle and tugged just hard enough to make sure the door wasn't locked. It budged effortlessly, with no resistance from the other side. Stacey pulled gently, opening the door with ease.

Inside was dark, so she slipped in and closed the door to avoid giving away her position. She crouched low and let her eyes adjust to the darkness.

She was in a hallway of some sort. Metal grating was beneath her, emptiness for dozens of feet below her before a concrete floor. She was inside the workshop for the metal fabrication company. Large equipment was scattered all over the concrete floor. I-beams and other steel structures were stacked against one wall, some stretching nearly to the ceiling. They had to be thirty feet tall, maybe more.

One side of the workshop had two levels above the floor with other smaller pieces of equipment. Metal pieces were stacked in seemingly organized piles on the first level. The other level was full of silent equipment.

Stacey moved forward, stepping slowly so the metal grating didn't echo with each step she took. Rooms that looked like offices were on both sides of her, all along the wall. The rest of the space was open for work to be done.

Stacey checked Vera's phone and saw the dot for Oscar was to her left. It hadn't moved in almost thirty minutes, but Stacey hoped he was still there.

She checked around the edge of the wall for anyone coming and wondered why she never thought to have a weapon before. Even a taser would have been better than absolutely nothing. Or self-defense classes. She needed both if she made it out of the building.

Stacey moved down the hall, looking at the other empty offices as she passed by them. The place was eerily quiet, even for a Saturday morning.

The first office was locked and dark. The second was dark, unlocked, but empty. The third office had a light on.

Stacey didn't want to surprise any unsuspecting people, so she looked through the blinds on the door to see if she could spot anyone inside. The office appeared to be empty, so she turned the knob on the door as quietly as possible, sighing with relief when it spun freely.

The door released with a soft click. Stacey held tight to the knob, easing the door open. She peeked through the opening and saw no one. She was about to close the door and leave when she paused and looked again. The other offices were completely dark. They looked like no one had been in them all day. But this one had a light on.

Stacey opened the door wider and considered what she was doing. She was looking for Oscar. She had no idea why he would be in that building, but she wasn't going to walk away without trying to find him. The app said he'd be close to that office. What if he was hiding inside? Stacey couldn't just walk away.

She checked out in the hallway again, but everything was just as silent as before. She walked into the office and closed the door behind her. The light was on the edge of the desk, shining a circle on the blond wood surface. Stacey moved closer, looking around as she made her way to the desk.

Oscar could be hiding behind the desk, or under it. He could be in another office. Hell, he could have stashed his phone in one of the desk drawers and not be there at all.

She had to stay focused. She was there to help Vera and get justice for Holly. Finding Oscar would also mean helping the women he moved in the van and two men he attacked the night before. He was not the kind of person who needed to be walking the street freely. He was dangerous. And he needed to be stopped.

Stacey listened for someone else's breath or movement, but she heard nothing. She moved closer to the desk, holding her own breath so she didn't make more noise than necessary. She reached the desk, moving to the side to check under it, and she froze.

Oscar was on the floor. A puddle of blood circled around him. Two puddles. His wrists were cut, the blood no longer pulsing out of him but oozing like he'd been there for a while and it was no longer his heart that pushed the blood out but gravity finishing the job.

Stacey stared at his lifeless eyes, hating that he was going to get away with all the things he did. She wanted him to pay. And suicide wasn't enough for him. It was too easy for the kind of man he was.

Oscar deserved to sit in jail for the rest of his life and think about what he did to Holly. Think about his daughter.

Think about the others he hurt. But instead, he was gone. Dead.

Stacey backed away from his body, not paying attention to where she was going. She bumped the edge of the desk with her hip, and something clattered to the floor. She bent to pick it up and set it back on the desk.

Suddenly, the lights came on in the office, blinding Stacey with their brightness.

"Freeze! Police!"

She threw her hands up, only then realizing the thing she picked up was a bloody knife. She let go of it, tossing it toward the police officers who had their guns trained on her.

"Don't move!"

One of the officers came closer to Stacey, his gun pointed right at her. She was too scared to move, or breathe. She wanted to cry, but she couldn't even do that. She just stood stock still.

The officer approached Stacey and put his gun away. Then he pulled out his cuffs and snapped them on her wrists. Tight. He pushed past her and stopped. He looked up at his partner. "Found him."

The other officer put his gun away and moved around the other side of the desk. He took his radio from his belt and called it in.

"Code four. Suspect in custody. Fugitive down. Need an ambulance to our location."

Suspect? The word trickled through Stacey's mind until it finally registered.

"You have the right to remain silent..." the officer said.

"Wait, no. I didn't do this. I didn't kill him. I'm innocent."

"You have the right to an attorney..."

"No. Please. This is a mistake. I found him in here."

"You're telling us you just happened to walk into this man's office and found him dead?"

"His office? What do you mean, his office?"

The officers exchanged a glance, and the one continued, "If you cannot afford an attorney..."

Oh my God. She was going to jail.

18

———

WRAY WAS ALREADY ON HIS WAY WHEN STACEY'S TWENTY minutes were up. He hated to sit back and let her go after this guy alone, but he had to trust her. That didn't mean he was going to like it or not follow her.

He parked behind her vehicle on the street and stared at it. She hadn't called him back. He wanted to be patient, but it wasn't his strong suit.

He dialed Marcus first. If Stacey was in trouble, Wray didn't want to call her and make her situation worse.

"Yeah?" Marcus answered.

"Marcus, it's Wray. Listen, you're not going to like this, but Stacey went after that guy you're looking for. Oscar something. I think she needs help."

"Fuck. That's not good news. Where is she?"

"She's at a metal fab place by the river."

"When did she get there?" Marcus's voice went deadly still.

"Thirty-six minutes ago. Why?"

"Because we have a team there right now."

"What? How did you know he'd be there?"

"He works there. Stacey had to have known that, too."

"She... I... I'm not sure. Do you think he's there?"

"The team is already on site. I'll check in with them and get back to you."

"I can't let her handle this alone. She's— Oh, shit." Wray yanked the handle and scrambled out of the truck.

"Wray, what's going on? Where are you?"

"She's in handcuffs, Marcus. They're arresting her." Wray ran down the street toward his wife as she was led by an officer around the building. "What the hell is going on?"

"Wray, stop," Marcus shouted into the phone. "I'll find out what's happening. They'll arrest you, too, if you get in the way."

"She's my fucking wife, Marcus."

"Wray—"

Wray ended the call and didn't hear the rest of what Marcus said. It didn't matter. He was not going to let them arrest Stacey.

"What is going on?" Wray shouted, finally getting the attention of the police officer manhandling his wife.

"Who the hell are you?" the cop barked, putting himself between Stacey and Wray.

"I'm her husband. And a firefighter. Why is she in handcuffs?"

"We found your wife standing over a body with a weapon in her hand."

Wray's heart sank. She couldn't have done it. She said she wanted him to pay for what he did, but she couldn't have killed him. Right?

"Stacey?" His voice pleaded with her to argue, to tell him it wasn't true. He needed to hear it from her. To know his wife wouldn't actually kill a man, no matter how bad that man was.

"She's already been read her rights. I would suggest she not say anything right now."

Wray ignored the cop and stared at his wife. She was still dressed like she was that morning when she left in jeans and a dark tee. Her sneakers were black, and she wore a mask he'd never seen before. She didn't look innocent. And the blazing look in her eyes said she might not be.

Stacey turned away from him and let the officer guide her into the back of the SUV. She stared up at Wray through the window. He just closed his eyes and prayed she was innocent.

No one would tell Wray anything at the police station. Stacey sat in the back of the SUV for at least thirty minutes before another cop came out of the surrounded building and joined the first cop. Wray followed them to the station and asked to see his wife, but they refused. He asked for information, and again they refused.

Wray had no idea what to do. He wanted to march in there and demand someone talk to him, but he knew that would only make things worse for both of them. So, he sat on his hands and tried not to panic about his wife going to jail for killing a murderer.

He checked his phone about a thousand times, waiting and willing for Marcus to call him and let him know what the hell was going on. He texted Braden to make sure the boys were okay and got the reply that they didn't know anything was different.

Wray hated feeling useless. He shouldn't have let Stacey go alone. He should have gone with her. Or called Marcus earlier. Or something. Anything. Stacey couldn't have killed that man. She wouldn't. She protected people, not hurt them.

But he killed her friend.

Wray shook the thought away. It didn't matter. Stacey wasn't the kind of person who would do that. There had to be an explanation for what the police saw.

Wray's leg bounced with nervous energy the longer he sat in the hard plastic chair and waited for someone to talk to him. He checked the time again. He'd been there almost two hours. Which meant Stacey was there that long. She'd been in handcuffs even longer. It wasn't right.

His phone finally rang. He jumped up to answer it when he saw Frannie's name on the screen. "Do you know anything?"

"I don't, Wray. I only know she's been arrested. But you know Stacey wouldn't hurt anyone."

"I know. That's not who she is."

"Good. Keep that faith. Marcus can't tell me anything, but I wanted to check on you and the boys."

"Braden's with them. I'm at the station."

"Oh, I'm so sorry. I didn't know you were working today."

"No, the police station. I followed Stacey here. No one will tell me anything."

"It's a Saturday. They might not let her out until she can see a judge on Monday morning."

"Are you fucking kidding me? She's innocent. She shouldn't be in jail for two nights."

"I agree, but our justice system is not always fair."

Wray scrubbed a hand over his face, the stubble on his jaw scratchy against his palm. He couldn't let his wife sit in jail for days.

"I need to go, Frannie. Thanks for calling. Oh, how's the kid?"

Frannie sighed. "Not good. Marcus came here to tell her about her dad. She's been a puddle since."

"Understandable."

"Yeah. But hard to watch."

"If you hear anything…"

"I'll be in touch. Keep the faith, Wray."

"Thanks, Frannie. You too."

"I always do."

Wray hung up and had to admit he felt better talking to Frannie. She had a calming effect on people. Even if he didn't like what she had to say.

Another hour passed before Marcus came out looking for Wray.

Wray started to ask questions, but Marcus silenced him with a look. Wray followed him without another word, looking around the station. Marcus led Wray to an interrogation room and closed the door behind them.

"What the hell is going on?"

STACEY JUMPED every time there was a noise outside the room they stuck her in. Footsteps, someone tapping on the wall, the slam of a door. It all tripped her pulse from scared to terrified.

She had no idea how she was going to get out of there. She was still in handcuffs, and she had a bad feeling she was going to stay that way for a long time.

Eventually, the single door in the room opened. Marcus strode in, and Stacey's shoulders sagged with relief. Then another man followed him and sat across from her.

"Marcus, what's going on?" Stacey asked.

"You're going to speak to me, not him," the man across from her said.

"Who are you?"

"Detective Harris."

"Why can't I talk to Marcus?"

Detective Harris glanced over his shoulder. He turned back to Stacey and scowled at her. "Captain Patrick shouldn't even be in the room right now, since he has a personal relationship with you. He is prohibited from asking you questions or addressing you, and you him. If neither of you will follow this rule, I will ask Captain Patrick to leave."

Stacey implored Marcus with a gaze, but he simply shook his head curtly. Stacey sighed, her entire body sinking with defeat.

"And?"

"Yes, I agree," Stacey mumbled.

"Sir?"

"I agreed before we walked in here, Detective," Marcus growled at the man.

Stacey wasn't sure if that was good or bad. Marcus was a teddy bear, but he could be a grizzly if he didn't like someone. His tone put Stacey on edge.

"Good. Thank you both. Now, Mrs. Allen, please tell me what you were doing in at Falls Metalworks today."

"I was looking for Oscar Hyatt."

"Why?"

Stacey hesitated. Would the truth make her look more or less guilty?

"Just tell the truth, Stacey," Marcus said.

"Sir," Detective Harris growled.

Stacey looked up at Marcus. He nodded, and she knew the only option was to tell the truth.

"I was called around three o'clock this morning by Oscar's daughter, Vera, to come get her from here. We were escorted to her home to collect some things for her, then I took her to the shelter where I work."

"The same one that Captain Patrick's wife owns?"

Stacey nodded. "Yes. I helped Vera get inside and get settled, then I talked to Frannie for a few minutes. She encouraged me to go home and rest and shower. I was going to do that when I realized Vera's phone was in my car."

The detective leaned back in his seat and crossed his arms. His shirt was pressed and neat. When he leaned back, creases from where he tucked it in streaked up the front, shattering the perfect image she had of the man. He was less intimidating with flaws. Which meant she was less scared.

"Vera had texts and calls, and when I went to see if anything was important, I saw her Find My Friends app."

"You knowingly violated the privacy of a minor," Detective Harris said.

"The minor in question was in my care. Even though her mother is dead, and her father was missing, I wanted to make sure there wasn't anyone else looking for her."

"And then you went through her phone."

"I wanted to find her father. So did the police, if you remember."

"Yes, but we wanted to find him alive."

"So did I!"

Detective Harris snorted. Marcus cleared his throat loudly. The detective drew a slow breath and leaned forward again. "Then what happened?"

Stacey told him about finding Oscar's phone signal and following it. She explained how she went into the building to look for him and make sure he was there before she notified the police, and then she found his body.

"Was he still alive when you found him?" Detective Harris asked.

"No. I mean, I don't think so. He didn't look like he was. I didn't check for a pulse or anything."

"So, you're claiming you did not kill Oscar Hyatt?"

"Yes. I did not kill Oscar Hyatt. Or anyone else you want to try to pin on me."

"Have you found any other dead bodies today, Mrs. Allen?" Detective Harris asked with a smirk.

"No," Stacey said, realizing how her words sounded. "I did not. Just Oscar Hyatt."

"When you found his body, what did you do?"

"I left. I tried to. I wasn't sure if anyone else was in the building, and I didn't know who killed Oscar, so I was going to leave and call Marcus when I got back to my car."

"Where did you get the knife?"

"It fell off the desk. When I turned to leave, my hip hit the desk, and it fell. I picked it up to set it on the desk again, and that's when the officers found me."

Detective Harris nodded slowly, considering her story. He rubbed his jaw and watched Stacey.

She fidgeted in her seat, hating the silence. She knew it was a tactic used by the police to make people talk. She used the same tactic, but she'd never been on the other side. She hadn't realized how uncomfortable it was.

"Did you go there with the intention of killing Oscar Hyatt?"

"No."

"Did you go there hoping to get revenge on him?"

"No."

"Did you bring that knife with you?"

"No!"

"Did you kill him?"

"No. I did not."

"Would you have if he wasn't dead when you showed up?"

"No. I just wanted to make sure he didn't get away. He killed his wife. He killed someone last night. He was driving that van a few days ago that had those women in it and set the fire that killed the one woman in the warehouse. He's a bad man. He didn't deserve to be free."

"So, you decided to kill him so he would never be free again?"

"No. I did not kill him. Am I sorry he's dead? Not even a little bit. But did I do it? No. That's not who I am."

Detective Harris leaned back and smiled. Marcus closed his eyes and shook his head. Stacey just looked between them.

"You had motive. And opportunity. I don't know how we can let her go, Captain," Detective Harris said.

"Let's talk outside," Marcus said.

Detective Harris raised an eyebrow at Stacey and smirked. Then he followed Marcus out the door.

Stacey stared at her hands. She knew he was trying to trick her into saying something, but she didn't see it coming. He was good. Even she was starting to think she was guilty. There was no way anyone else would believe she wasn't.

A few minutes later, the door opened again. That time, only Marcus walked in.

"What's going on?"

"You're free to go," Marcus said.

"What? How? Why?"

Marcus uncuffed her and helped her to stand. "The officers at the scene found a suicide note on the computer on Oscar's desk. They confirmed the fingerprints on the keys were Oscar's. There were no others. You weren't wearing gloves when the officers found you and there were no gloves found in your possession or anywhere else in the office, so there's no reason to assume there was any foul play on your part."

"He killed himself?" Stacey gasped.

Marcus nodded. "That's what it looks like. His wrists were cut, left deeper than the right since he's right-handed. There were smears of blood on the chair from where he appeared to have been when he cut himself. The knife you picked up is the only other thing in the room that had fingerprints that weren't Oscar's."

"I promise you, Marcus, I didn't kill him. He was dead when I found him. I know I shouldn't have gone in there alone, but I couldn't stand the thought of him getting away again."

"It appears as though he couldn't either. He confessed to killing Holly in his suicide note."

"Oh, God," Stacey breathed. She leaned forward, relief and sadness overwhelming her. Tears immediately sprang to her eyes. She shook with a sob that she couldn't hold back.

Marcus rubbed her back. He got it. He knew Holly, too. He knew all of them. It wasn't often someone from Shelter in the Storm was lost, but when it happened, it was hard on all of them.

"I can't believe it. I knew it, but I never thought we'd prove it."

"He confessed to a lot of things in his letter. I guess his conscience finally got the best of him."

"That doesn't sound like him. I wonder why."

Marcus shook his head. "I don't know, but I'm happy Holly can finally rest in peace."

"Me, too."

Marcus squeezed Stacey's hand. "Come on. There's someone here to see you."

Stacey followed Marcus out of the room and into another one. Before she walked in, Wray said, "Marcus, what the hell— Stacey!"

Stacey hurried over to him and threw herself into his arms. He caught her easily and pressed his nose against her neck.

"Are you okay? Are you free? What happened?"

"She's free," Marcus answered for her. "Apparently, it was a suicide. Oscar confessed in his note about all the things he's done. Stacey was in the wrong place at the wrong time. Breaking and entering is something the owner of the company can decide on, but since she didn't actually break in, I doubt they'll press charges."

"Are you okay?" Wray repeated. He cupped her jaw and lifted her face to his. He pressed their foreheads together and looked her over.

Stacey nodded. "I'm okay. Scared, hungry, tired. And heartbroken for Vera."

"Let's get you home so you can shower and change and then go back to the shelter to see her."

"Are you sure?" Stacey asked.

Wray nodded. "Of course. I think she needs you right now. And I think maybe you need her, too."

Stacey smiled up at him. "I'm so lucky to have you in my life."

"Feeling's mutual."

19

Frannie was sitting in the front room when Stacey got back to Shelter in the Storm. Stacey went in and sat with her, hugging her tight.

"Are you okay?" Frannie asked.

Stacey nodded. "I am. It wasn't fun to get arrested, but I told them the truth."

"I know. Marcus called. He said Oscar committed suicide."

Stacey shrugged. "I guess. It seems too easy, but I don't know. Maybe he couldn't handle everything he did. I hate to say it, but the world is better without someone like him in it."

Frannie nodded. "True, but one little girl might not see things the same way."

"Have you spoken to her?"

Frannie shook her head. "I knew you'd want to be here."

"Thank you. Do you want to come with me?"

"Of course."

Frannie led the way upstairs and down the hall to the room Stacey left Vera in that morning. It was hard to believe only a few hours had passed when it felt like a lifetime. Stacey hated that she had to tell Vera she'd lost another parent, and that he confessed to killing her mom. She would learn the truth eventually, and hearing it from Stacey would be easier. Not that it would ever be easy.

Frannie knocked on Vera's door and waited until the girl called out for her to enter. Frannie peeked her head in, smiling and asking Vera if they could talk.

"Yeah, sure," Vera said, her voice muffled and unsteady.

Stacey walked in behind Frannie and noted how small Vera looked. She was curled up on the bed with her arms wrapped around her knees. Her eyes were rimmed with red, and her cheeks were splotchy. The collar of her gray tee was wet.

Stacey and Frannie went to opposite sides of the twin bed and both sat on the edge. They exchanged a glance before Frannie nodded for Stacey to take the lead.

"We wanted to talk to you about today," Stacey said.

Vera drew in a shaky breath and let it out unevenly. The pain she felt was nothing compared to what she was about to feel, and Stacey's heart broke for the girl. She was too young to know the sort of pain she was about to face.

"Did the police find my dad?"

Stacey nodded. "They did, honey. And I'm sorry, but he was already dead when they found him."

"No!" she cried. Sobs shook her body, and she ducked her head to rest on her knees. "He can't be dead, too. He can't!"

Stacey and Frannie moved to sit next to Vera and held her as she cried. Stacey knew from the sessions they had that Vera adored her father as much as she didn't trust him. She'd seen enough that she knew he had a mean streak, but he doted on her and confused her. It didn't matter that he was evil, he was still her dad. And losing him was going to be something she would have to deal with for the rest of her life.

"I'm so sorry, sweetheart," Frannie said soothingly. "I know how hard this is for you."

"How would you know?" Vera asked, her tone sharp and biting.

Stacey assumed it was something Frannie was saying to make Vera feel better, but her friend and boss started to talk.

"My father was like yours. He was abusive to my mother. Never in front of me, but I knew what was going on. When she couldn't handle it, he came after me. I tried to fight back, but that only made things worse, so I learned to let him get it out of his system."

"I didn't know," Vera breathed. "My dad never hit me, though." She averted her gaze. "I knew he hit my mom. I didn't help her."

"There was nothing you could have done to help her, honey," Frannie said. "With men like that, very little gets through to them."

"Did anything get through to your dad?"

Frannie shook her head. A haunted look crossed her face, one that made Stacey's heart clench before Frannie continued her story.

"My dad was one of the bad ones. He wasn't willing to see that what he was doing was wrong. The only thing that stopped him was death."

"Your mom killed him?"

Frannie shook her head. "No. He killed my mom, then killed himself. I was thirteen."

"Oh, my God," Vera breathed.

"It wasn't an easy time for me, but I knew it meant my mother was no longer suffering. And neither was my father.

I don't know what demons he had in him, but he had some. I don't think I'll ever completely forgive what he did, but I've accepted that he wasn't well."

"I need to know something," Vera said, her voice stronger even as it wobbled.

Stacey and Frannie nodded for Vera to continue.

"Did my dad kill my mom?"

Stacey put her hand on Vera's arm and drew the girl's attention. She waited until Vera looked up at her and saw in Vera's eyes that she already knew the truth.

"Yes. He did," Stacey said simply. There was no way to make it easier to hear.

Vera nodded. A single tear slid down her cheek. "I hate him for that."

"And you have every right to hate him," Frannie said. "He took her from you. All she was doing was trying to protect both of you, but he took her. It's going to take you time to fully process all of this, but you're strong and smart. And we will be here for you anytime you need us."

Vera drew a breath and pressed her lips up into a tentative smile. "Thank you." She paused and looked across the room, then asked, "Do you know how my dad died?"

"He committed suicide," Stacey said.

"No. There's no way," Vera argued instantly.

"Excuse me?"

"He wouldn't have done that. His dad killed himself. He told me it was a coward's way out. He hated his father for doing it. That's not true. The police are lying." Vera pushed her way off the bed and paced back and forth.

Stacey and Frannie stood with her, standing on opposite sides of the bed. Stacey's mind spun with questions she didn't have answers to. She thought back over what the room looked like when she walked in. She didn't see Oscar's body until she walked around the desk. He was lifeless, slumped onto the floor.

But the knife was on the desk. On the edge of the desk, because it fell when she bumped the desk.

If Oscar set it down on the desk, there would have been blood there. And all over the chair. Unless he was standing, but that seemed unlikely.

"Where's Marcus? I want to talk to him," Vera declared.

"He's at work, but I'll call him and see when he can get here," Frannie said. "But, honey, you need to know, your father left a note. He typed it into his computer."

"The only fingerprints on the keys were his," Stacey added. She had to convince herself, too.

"No. He wouldn't have done it. I know it. He would never."

Stacey and Frannie worked to calm Vera down. The only thing that helped was Frannie calling Marcus and him promising to be there soon to talk to Vera.

She finally settled on the bed again. The vacant look in her eyes wasn't a good one, but she needed to go through the different stages of grief.

"I'd like to tell you something else," Stacey said.

Vera nodded.

"That necklace your dad gave you? It's not similar to your mom's. It is your mom's."

"What are you talking about?"

"A friend of mine had that necklace custom-made for her. It's the only one that exists."

"How did he...? Oh, my God." She broke down in tears and curled onto her side. It was like she was holding out hope that Oscar didn't really kill Holly, but that information shattered it.

Frannie and Stacey sat with Vera while she cried again.

When she calmed down once more, they talked her into going downstairs to get something to eat and call her aunt. Holly's sister lived in Illinois. Holly talked about moving there once Vera was done with school. It seemed like the best option for Vera now.

Andrea said she'd be there the next day, and Vera was relieved to have that piece of her life settled. She ate a sandwich and drank some water, and they waited for Marcus to arrive.

The three of them were watching TV when Marcus walked in. He nodded to Vera, and all of them moved into Frannie's office so they had privacy to talk.

"Frannie told me what you said," Marcus started. "I promise you, we are going to look into every possibility."

"He would never do that. I don't care what the letter said, it's not possible. Someone else killed him," Vera insisted.

"If that's true, we will find out who," Marcus promised her.

Fear slithered up Stacey's spine. She couldn't explain it, but she believed Vera. She knew Oscar didn't kill himself. Or didn't do it willingly.

Which meant there was someone else out there who'd been pulling the strings. But who?

Stacey finally made it home late in the day. Braden's truck was gone, and lights were still on downstairs. She was exhausted, and all she wanted to do was eat and crash.

As soon as she opened the door, her stomach growled. Something delicious met her nose, drawing her to the kitchen where she found her three boys.

Wray came over and kissed her. "How did everything go?"

"As well as can be expected."

"I'm so sorry for her. To lose them both the way she did."

"You know what's crazy? Frannie's parents were the same. Dad killed mom, then himself." Stacey kept her voice low so Joey and Evan didn't hear what they were talking about.

"Wow. That's horrible."

Stacey nodded. "Yeah. But Vera's convinced her dad didn't kill himself. She said he never would because he sees suicide as weak."

"That's not true, though. It's painful and the people who take their own lives do it because they can't see any other way out. If everything was closing in on Oscar, he could have gotten to that point."

Stacey shrugged. "I agree, but I kind of believe her."

"Why?"

Stacey shook her head. "I can't really explain it, but I keep seeing him lying there. And where the knife was. It doesn't really make sense."

"You think someone killed him?"

"I don't know, but I think it's very possible."

"What's you talking about?" Evan asked loudly.

Stacey pushed away thoughts of Oscar and focused on her family. "I was telling Daddy how good dinner smells. What are we having?"

"Pasketti!" Evan shouted.

"Ooh, no wonder it smells so good. That's my favorite."

"Me, too," Evan agreed. He went back to coloring the workbook in front of him, his tongue sticking out of the side of his mouth.

Stacey walked over and hugged him, smiling when he

fought her hold so he could keep working. She moved to Joey next and looked at what he was doing, hugging him, too.

She hoped Vera would have a piece of that kind of life when she moved to be with her aunt. She deserved happiness after everything she'd been through. Stacey hoped she'd find it.

AFTER DINNER, they curled up on the couch together and watched a movie. The boys repeated half the lines of the family favorite. Stacey smiled and was grateful. It wasn't long ago she never thought her life would look like that again.

Wray took the boys upstairs to read a story after the movie. Stacey was tired, but she wanted to make sure the kitchen was cleaned up and the pots from spaghetti were soaking so they would be easy to clean in the morning. She was too tired to do it before bed.

She wiped down the table and the counters, then hung the dishrag to dry on the front of the stove. Stacey looked around once more as she listened to Wray reading to the boys.

She loved her life.

A knock on the backdoor made her jump. Their yard was fenced, and visitors used the front door. Who the hell would be at the back?

Stacey grabbed a knife from the block and tiptoed to the door. She put her hand on the knob and took a deep breath, trying to calm her racing heart.

The knock came again, this time with a voice. "Stacey? It's Jessica."

Stacey whipped the door open, setting the knife on the counter. "Jessica? What are you...? Is that blood?"

Jessica's hands shook as she tried to brush away the bloodstains on her jeans and tee. "Yeah. Sorry. I just—"

"Come in. Are you hurt? What the hell happened?"

Jessica shook her head. She looked around, her eyes wide with fear. "Do you have a way to get in touch with Raina?"

"Raina? Um, yeah, I have a number for her. Why? What's going on?"

"Karli's dead." Jessica's voice had zero emotion in it. Stiff. Wooden. Like it wasn't real.

"What? How? What?"

"I didn't do it, Stacey. I promise you. It wasn't me."

"Of course not. Why would I ever think that?"

Jessica exhaled deeply, like she expected Stacey to question her. "Karli sent me a text to come over earlier today. She wanted..." Jessica's lip wobbled. "I had a date with Braden last night, and Karli wanted to hear how it went. I was going over there earlier for dinner and movie night, but when I got there..."

Jessica doubled over, wrapping her arm around her stomach.

"Jessica, come inside. Let's get you cleaned up and into fresh clothes."

"No," she said sharply. "I can't. I just... Someone saw me there, I guess. I don't know. I called nine-one-one, but I kind of freaked out because the operator asked me why I killed someone, and I just left, but I was covered in blood, and someone must have seen me leaving Karli's apartment, and now the police have my name and face all over the news because they think I killed my friend, but I didn't, Stacey. I didn't kill her. She was dead when I got there. Her head…" Jessica reached back and touched the back of her skull. "Her head was smashed in, and blood was just everywhere, and oh, my God, Karli's dead. Stacey, she's dead."

"Jessica, please come in. We'll figure this out. I'll call Marcus, and—"

"No," Jessica barked. "I can't. I can't put your family in danger. I wouldn't have come here at all, except I was worried about Raina. I don't know where she'll go, or if she's okay. I don't know who killed Karli. It could have been Raina's husband trying to get to her. Or it could have been random. But Karli was so sweet, and I don't know why anyone would want to hurt her."

"We'll figure this out. Where are you staying?"

Jessica shook her head. "I don't know. And if I did, I wouldn't be able to tell you."

"Why not? I want to help you. Let me help you. Wray and Braden can help. Marcus. We'll—"

"I don't want to involve any of you. Braden… It's not fair to any of you. Just find Raina. Please. Make sure she's safe."

"I will. But Jessica, you don't have to do this alone. We can help you. You can stay at the shelter."

"Marcus lives there. He wouldn't be able to not turn me in."

"Well…" Stacey couldn't lie and say that wasn't true because it was. But she didn't like thinking of Jessica on her own.

"I know you want to help, and I appreciate it, but I just came here so you'd know to look for Raina. Okay?"

"Okay. Jessica—"

"Hey, Stace," Wray said from the front of the house. His footsteps on the stairs were getting closer. "Have you seen my phone?"

Stacey turned to answer him. "Um, no, but I'll help you look in a minute."

Stacey turned back to Jessica, but she was gone. Stacey stepped outside, hoping to catch sight of her, but the backyard was empty.

"Hey. What are you doing outside?" Wray asked.

"Um, Jessica was just here."

"Braden's Jessica?"

Stacey nodded. "Yeah. And she's in trouble."

Subscribe to my newsletter and receive Frannie and Marcus's story for free.

Sign up at

https://maryethompson.com/subscribe/

FRAMED IS COMING JULY 15...

After Jessica shows up at Stacey's, she disappears. She has no idea who killed her friend, and she has no idea how she's going to clear her name. All she knows is she had the best night of her life with Braden and the worst day of her life finding her friend's body, all within twenty-four hours. She can't have those be her last. But that means finding the truth, and getting justice.

Preorder FRAMED now!

MARY E THOMPSON
USA TODAY BESTSELLING AUTHOR
FREEDOM
F-BOMB: SEALs LOVE CURVES

Chapter One

The vibrating phone woke Archer Ford from a sound sleep. Well, as sound as his sleep ever was. He snatched it from the table next to his bed.

"What?"

A quick intake of breath on the other end of the line had the hairs on the back of his neck standing on end. He was on his feet, wide awake in seconds. Archer was ready for anything.

Or so he thought.

"Is this Archer?" the woman asked.

"Who is this?" he demanded. He never answered questions when he didn't know who was asking them.

"I need to know if I have the right number. Is this Archer Ford? Jaymes's brother?"

"How do you know my brother?" Archer asked, knowing he needed to get her talking if he was going to find out anything. He had a feeling in his gut, and his gut was never wrong. He just never expected the bad news to come from his brother.

"I'm his best friend. He told me to call you if I ever needed something. And I… I need your help. Well, really, he does. And I didn't know who to call or what to do. I'm really worried. He never does this sort of thing. Maybe I'm overreacting, but—"

"Stop talking," Archer barked.

She shut up instantly.

"Now, tell me what the hell you're talking about. What's going on? Who doesn't do what sort of thing?"

"Jaymes. He disappeared a few days ago, and I don't know where he is. He hasn't been answering his phone, and he didn't tell me he was leaving, and—"

"Stop! My brother is missing?" Dread sank into Archer and hooked on to every nerve in his body.

"Well, missing is such a strong word. Maybe he's working on a project and his phone died."

"Has he ever done that before?"

She sucked in a breath. "Jaymes? No."

"He's never gone off without telling you?"

"No. Never."

"Are you fucking my brother?"

She gasped. "Who the hell do you think you are to ask me something like that? That's none of your business!"

"So, no," Archer said. But she wants to.

Lucky bastard. Archer couldn't remember the last woman who wanted him. And the voice on the other end of his phone was sultry and seductive and could get him hard in an instant if she weren't telling him his brother was missing.

Not kidnapped, she said.

He rolled his eyes.

"Fine, no. I'm not sleeping with Jaymes. What does that have to do with anything?"

"Because I need to know how much you matter to my brother. If you're his girlfriend, whoever took him could come back for you to use as leverage. Where are you?"

"Do you really think they'd do that?" she whispered, her voice laced with fear.

Shit. Archer forgot he was talking to a civilian, not a fellow SEAL. Not that he could consider them his brothers any longer. He quit with the rest of them. He didn't want to go, but he wasn't given a choice like the others. Honorably discharged, they said. It meant the same fucking thing.

He was out. His career was over. There was nothing left for him.

"I don't know who 'they' are or what they're capable of, but anything is possible. If you're a friend and not his girlfriend, they might not care about you. If he really was kidnapped."

"His place was trashed. It looked like someone tossed it. That's the right word for it, right? When someone goes through looking for something?"

Archer nearly groaned. She was going to be a piece of work. "Yeah. Anyway. Stay where you are. I'll... be there in a few hours."

"What should I do if they come to get me?"

"Hide," Archer said, then hung up the phone.

He closed his eyes and took a deep breath. He had no desire to return home. He'd be happy if he never set foot in Western New York ever again. Hell, all of New York.

But he couldn't leave his brother. Especially when he had that feeling in his gut. Something wasn't right.

Archer pulled into his brother's parking lot around five in the morning. He was exhausted from driving all night, but he was on high alert. He slid his Glock into the back of his waistband and headed for the door to his brother's building.

The door was locked, but easy enough to get into. He slipped inside and looked around. He'd never been in the building before, but it was like any other apartment building. Dark carpet, beige walls, dim lighting, and that never-ending smell of lemon-scented cleaner that only masked the deeper scent of multiple people living under the same roof.

He checked the numbers on the first floor. He'd never been to his brother's apartment, thought he never would be, so he had no idea which floor he lived on. Unit 17 couldn't be too high up, but Archer really had no clue.

Three floors up, he finally found it at the back of the building. He quickly picked the lock and let himself inside, closing the door with a soft click.

The apartment was dark. Blinds were drawn against the sunlight that would try to spill inside in less than two hours. Archer waited, listening, as his eyes adjusted to the space.

He was in a small entryway. A boot tray was on his left, and jackets hung on the wall behind the door. There was a small table in front of him and a tiny kitchen farther off to the left. He crept around the table and peeked into the kitchen. Nothing seemed particularly out of place. No dishes in the sink and only a few small appliances on the counter, but nothing that concerned him.

He continued into the living room, glancing around. His brother was always neat, putting his toys away and keeping his room spotless. He was the son their dad didn't have to get after about every little thing. Not like Archer. Jaymes was perfect, and Archer was a fuck-up. It was the story of their lives.

The living room was clear, so Archer kept going toward a back hallway. He couldn't see around the corner, so he drew his gun. His hand shook. *Fuck.* He switched hands and shook it out. He closed his eyes for just a second, long enough to force his demons back into the grave where they belonged.

Archer swapped the gun to his right hand again and let it lead the way into the hall. A bathroom was right in front of him, and two bedrooms opened up a step farther into the darkness.

He took a step forward, going toward the bathroom, the easiest of the three to check, when he heard it. Nothing any normal person would pick up, but he wasn't normal. Hadn't been in far too long.

Breathing. Uneven. Fear or excitement? He didn't know.

Archer moved slowly, hoping he could catch the person off guard. He stopped his own breathing so he could just listen and pinpointed their position. In the first bedroom, the one directly across from the bathroom. Just inside the door. Probably either a gun or another weapon in hand if the person was waiting that close to the door.

He moved quickly once he knew where to go and stepped into the bedroom and pointed his gun right at the person's face.

A gasp. Then the shaky breath.

Definitely not someone threatening. Jaymes's girlfriend, maybe?

"Who are you and what are you doing here?"

"I'm Lily Scott," she whimpered. "I was just—"

"You're the one from the phone," Archer said, lowering his gun. "The best friend."

She sagged onto the bed, her whole body shaking. She drew her knees up to her chest and wrapped her arms around them and tried to suck in breath after breath.

Archer crouched down in front of her. The last thing he needed was her having a panic attack. "Breathe with me. Slow, deep breaths. Count to three. In, two, three. Out, two, three. In, two, three. Out, two, three."

To his surprise, she did what he said. She stared into his eyes and dragged in one ragged breath after another until there wasn't a hitch in each one.

"Feeling better?" he asked.

She nodded. "I think so. Um, who are you?"

His dark eyebrows shot up, and he almost laughed. She just sat there with him, after he pointed a gun in her face, and had no idea who he was? "You called me. I'm Archer."

Her eyes scanned him until the appraisal drove him to

his feet. He didn't want to know what she saw when she looked at him. Especially not with the darkness that hung between them. In the harsh light of day, it would be a different story, but in the dark, Archer couldn't hide from the truth in the dark.

He smacked the switch and flooded the room with too much light. He let his eyes adjust for a second, then took a good look at the woman who asked for his help.

Jesus, she was beautiful.

She wore the tiniest pair of shorts he'd ever seen and a tank top that was so tight it might as well have been see-through. Not that he was complaining. Pink was definitely his new favorite color. Pink shorts, pink top, and pink nipples trying to peek out and say hi.

He was *up* to the task.

"I didn't think you could get here so fast. What time is it?"

"Five. You said my brother was missing. I thought this was his place, so I came here."

"It is," Lily said quickly.

Archer scanned the room, taking in the rumpled queen sized bed, the woman's clothes tossed around, and the mix of items that had to be his brother's and there was only one conclusion to draw. Lily might not be screwing his brother, but they were doing something.

"You live here, too?"

Lily shook her head. "No. I have my own place, but you said to stay put. I figured if Jaymes came home during the night, I could call you and let you know he was back. I didn't realize you were going to be here already."

Archer nodded and looked around. He didn't know his brother well. Not anymore. Once upon a time they were close, but that ended years ago, when Archer was ten and his brother was only six. It had been years since Archer had even seen Jaymes, let alone knew anything about his life. He was pretty sure Jaymes did something with computers, but what, he had no clue.

"Do you stay here often?" Archer asked for some unknown reason. It was obvious she was close to Jaymes, whether they were involved or not. She was at risk if Jaymes really was kidnapped. How often she spent the night was only relevant to the side of him that was trying to decide if he could sleep with her and not piss off his brother.

Lily shrugged, shifting her breasts and dragging his gaze back to them. They jiggled a bit when she moved. Even more when she talked. She liked to talk with her hands. Hell, she talked with her whole body. Her hips swayed gently as she spoke, and her hair, brown with blonde and red strung through it, curved around her breasts like lovers caressing her.

He was jealous of her damn hair.

"Are you even listening to me?" she asked, hands punching those sexy hips.

Archer shook his head. "Long drive."

Her irritation slid away, and genuine concern replaced it. "I'm sorry. I didn't even think about that. Can I make you some coffee? Or maybe you prefer tea. We have water and orange juice. Do you want breakfast?"

"Lily," Archer said loudly to get her attention. She'd already moved into the kitchen and flipped on every light in the apartment. Pans banged under a cabinet as she bent at the waist to retrieve them.

His brother was a damn saint if he wasn't sleeping with this woman.

"Eggs? How about an omelet? I make a killer omelet.

Jaymes loves my... omelets." She turned watery eyes up to Archer. "Am I ever going to see him again?"

Archer couldn't think about that. Losing his brother wasn't an option. He'd lost too many of them during his time as a SEAL. He wasn't going to lose the only one he actually shared DNA with.

"You'll see him again," he promised Lily. "I'll find him."

She fell into his arms like she'd run out of energy to keep herself upright. Adrenaline was a bitch. One minute Lily was getting ready to make breakfast, and the next she was crashing in Archer's arms.

He held her awkwardly. It had been a while since he'd touched a woman, let alone had one in his arms. And the last time, she was definitely not crying. Screaming, panting, and moaning, yeah, but not crying.

She clung to him for a few seconds, long enough that his cock took notice of the curvy, warm woman in his arms. She smelled like every good thing the world had to offer. Like cookies and fresh air and woman all rolled into one. He wanted to press his face into her neck and inhale her deep, but he had no right. She belonged to Jaymes.

"I'm sorry," she said, taking a big step back. "I know you don't like people to lean on you. I just lost it. I've been so scared, you know. And I feel so much better with you here. Jaymes always said you could do anything, and I believe it. I know you'll find him and bring him back. And I really appreciate it."

Archer's mind spun with the load she dropped on him. Obviously, his brother talked about him. And it wasn't good.

The only problem was it was all true. He wasn't the kind of guy a person could lean on. He wasn't reliable. He always managed to fuck things up one way or another. He was there because he owed it to Jaymes. Archer had been trying to repay his brother for years, and this was his first opportunity. When he found him and returned him to his woman, Archer could crawl back in his hole and disappear again.

"Uh, yeah. I'll find him."

"Thank you," Lily said.

Her smile gutted him. She had faith in him. She trusted him. He didn't deserve either, but he'd do his best to deliver for her. A woman like her deserved to be happy. And if Jaymes made her happy, Archer would give up his own life to save him. It was the least he owed, to Jaymes and to Rodney.

"If I'm going to find him, I need some information from you. Tell me everything you know. About my brother, what he does, where he spends his time, everything. You're the only lead I have right now, so I need your help."

Read FREEDOM today

ABOUT THE AUTHOR

USA TODAY Bestselling Author Mary E Thompson spent most of her childhood wishing she had a few less curves. She hid in the pages of books because her favorite characters never cared what size her clothes were. Now, neither does Mary, and she writes stories that celebrate women like her. Real women who have curves, chase dreams, and find love, because we should all be happy, no matter our dress size.

Mary spends her non-writing time with her husband and two kids, watching too much TV, cheering for her hometown football team (Go Bills!), and hiding chocolate from her family.

Visit https://MaryEThompson.com/subscribe/ to sign up for Mary's newsletter, **Romancing the Curves**. Subscribers get free ebooks and other fun stuff, like exclusive, members only content and giveaways, plus are the first to know about new releases and sales!